Ron Johnson

Death on the Withlacoochee

Written By: **Ron Johnson**

Copyright © 2006 by Ron Johnson

ISBN 0-7414-2984-5

Published by:

INFI(∞)ITY
PUBLISHING.COM

1094 New DeHaven Street, Suite 100
West Conshohocken, PA 19428-2713
Info@buybooksontheweb.com
www.buybooksontheweb.com
Toll-free (877) BUY BOOK
Local Phone (610) 941-9999
Fax (610) 941-9959

Printed in the United States of America

Printed on Recycled Paper

Published January 2006

Prolog

The River

The early mist had settled and the fishing slowed as the sun sent tiny glitters through the overhanging trees. He caught a few fish that morning but still anticipated the adrenalin rush of a big bass exploding the water. His empty stomach wrestled with these expectations as he drifted in search of that perfect spot to make just one more cast before returning to his home on the river for breakfast. The river cast its spell and lulled him into that sublime state of reflection, where the sheer beauty could keep him there forever in spite of the hunger or lack of a fighting fish on the end of his line. The pale green lace of the cypress leaves shimmered in the glint of morning sunlight in contrast with dark stately trunks rising from even darker water. Cypress knees like pawns protecting royalty, stood guard at their base while wisps of ghost gray moss decorated their boughs.

A sound reached his ears that brought him out of his trance. Being several miles away, he could not yet feel the vibrations he knew were to come. He listened to the sound grow steadily and resigned himself to the coming disruption of his peaceful communion with nature. The sound grew from a distant buzz to a throaty rumble then erupted into a deafening roar while still around two bends upriver. He stubbornly kept fishing in an effort to convince himself, that he wouldn't let it get to him this time. After all, he thought sarcastically, they sometimes slow down when they spot someone and idle by before blasting away again, leaving behind the smell of exhaust in the air and the clutter of debris blown into the water.

I

He caught the look of surprise on the air boater's face, as he rounded the bend at cruising speed, saw him, and cut his throttle quickly. The air boater's surprised look grew into a placid smile as he passed, throwing a tremendous wake, plowing through the water just below planning speed. Shouts for him to slow down didn't change that placid smile a bit, for how could the air boater hear him with those earmuffs he wore? For that matter, he couldn't hear himself hollering at the air boater, with eight cylinders of un-muffled raw power pounding his own ears. He held the gunnel with one hand and his fishing hat with the other, anticipating the air blast to come. The small fishing boat lurched as the wake hit and nearly threw him overboard. He grabbed for the other gunnel to brace himself, and as the airboater hit the throttle again, the prop wash blew his hat into the water. He nearly capsized the boat retrieving the hat, and then just sat there in an unbelieving stupor, while the rush of air and noise receded downriver.

The fishing was over, the mood gone. The debris blown in the water from the air blast would foul his lures on every cast. It would be some time until the current washed the trash ashore and the river returned to normal. He wondered how this could be allowed to happen. He wondered what sort of mentality it took to invade this beautifully serene setting with a malevolent machine that consumed the environment for miles. Even its distant buzz disturbed the solitude with the anticipation of a monstrous presence transforming this quiet stream into a noisy wind tunnel.

Mike Tracy vowed to change things.

Chapter One

Just one more cast

Jimmy Thompson cut the throttle and drifted with the current in the middle of the river. The late evening sun penetrated the dense growth of cypress along the banks and cast long shadows across the water. The smooth surface of the tannin stained water reflected the image of the cypress knees that stood like sentinel guards before the royalty of the stately trees. Spanish moss shrouded the overhanging limbs of the two hundred year old giants. He never tired of the river. It was not only the fishing that he loved, it was the quiet beauty, and the peaceful aura that he knew belied the sinister undertones, the undertones of wildlife struggling for survival. He loved the eerie feeling he had at night when the large gators bellowed and grunted to warn trespassers, their eyes staring, unblinking, reflecting red in the flashlight beam. He only went out on the river at night with Grandpa Jim or Captain Mike. He couldn't wait for Captain Mike to take him gator hunting.

Jimmy, in a lot of ways was a typical teenager, the man inside struggling to emerge and gain independence, but his small frame, tousled red hair peeking out from the edges of his grandpa's old fishing hat, and the freckles on his fair skin would give him a youthful appearance far into manhood. Both the teenager and the man in Jimmy would fish until well after dark. It was the boy that made the promise to his grandmother, but the man intended to keep it. He knew Granny would scold him if he came in after dark, even if he did have a stringer full of fish. She didn't want him on the river at night; she had told him that just this afternoon. She had said, "You know how fast those airboats run. Some of 'em don't slow down much after dark. They could run right over you, and leave you for gator bait. You be home before dark young man," and he had said he would. He had no fear of the river, but knew Granny was right. After all, his little fishing boat had no running lights and the faded gray of its plywood sides was hard to see, especially tonight, when there would be no moon to light the river. Jimmy looked at his watch, his prize possession, his legacy from his father. It was one of the few tangible things remaining after the death of his mother and father in a tragic and senseless automobile accident. He realized it would be close; there wasn't much daylight left.

After his parents were gone and he moved in with Granny and Gramps, as he called them, he became conscious of Granny's deep sorrow at the loss of her son and her outsized fear of anything happening to him. He knew and understood why she was so overprotective. She was never unreasonable, but he often saw the unspoken anguish when she gently chided him for being overdue. She never yelled at him, that would have hurt him less. The sting of sharp words spoken in anger would incite him to defensive anger. She knew how to get the most out of her words. Jimmy idolized his grandparents and respected their authority.

He still thought at times about that phone call two years ago as he and his grandparents were watching a late movie. Grandpa Jim answered and just said yes a few times, glanced at him then looked at Grandma Jenny with a strange vacancy in his eyes. Jimmy saw the color drain from her sun tanned face, and her hand went to her mouth as if to suppress something awful. It was as if she knew everything that grandpa had heard on the phone. Jimmy hadn't caught on yet. He only knew something was very wrong. She reached out for him and held him to her breast, with Gramps still holding her tear filled gaze locked to his, as if they were talking out loud to each other.

His parents had left him in their care for the summer earlier that evening and then left for their home in Clearwater. They never arrived, and he never saw them again, not even what was left of them at the funeral. At almost twelve years, he was old enough to know about automobile accidents and suspect the devastation they could have on the victims or their survivors, but he never suspected it could hurt so much.

His grandparents took him in after the accident and they helped each other back from the devastating loss. He knew the

2

hurt in their hearts was as great as his. He somehow knew he had taken his father's place in their life and that his Grandma's fussing about the dangers of the river, openly expressed her very real fears, of losing him as well. He had made a promise to her and would try to keep it.

He had only been fishing a couple of hours and had three keeper bass and a couple of nice pan-fish on the stringer, just one more hot spot on his agenda, around the next bend, where the bass come in at dusk, to feed in the shallow area. The swifter current there would sweep him by quickly, with only a few chances to cast his lures, so he wanted to have his boat in the right position.

He heard the distant thunder of an airboat motor starting upriver. "Aw hell!" he said out loud, "He must be at the spring." He knew the airboat would ruin the fishing, if it came his way. He hated the monstrous machines. You could hear them coming two miles away, the big V8 engines with no mufflers, their props beating the wind. The drivers wore earmuffs or earplugs to protect their ears. He wondered if the ones who didn't have the courtesy to slow down thought everyone wore earmuffs on the river? Captain Mike hated them too, he said they ought to be banned from the river; the river was too small for boats that fast.

Jimmy was anxious to see which direction the airboat came. If it came his way the heavy wake would wash the shallow area muddy and the prop blast would blow the leaves and trash into the water for his lures to foul on. *And besides that, it's gettin' dark fast,* he thought. He wouldn't have time to let things settle down after the airboat passed. He decided to wait—if it did come his way, the fishing would be over anyway and he would scurry on home, if not he could make a few casts and still keep his promise to Granny.

He drifted around the bend, caught a branch on the submerged tree that had fallen in the last spring flood. The huge root system had pulled an even bigger chunk of the bank away, a chunk large enough to anchor the two hundred year old giant from being swept on down the river. The trunk lay just under the surface, the limbs above water dried and scaled with dead leaves and bark, the limbs below reached deep into the dark water, supporting the massive trunk which had been cut off at mid stream to allow boats to pass on the inside of the bend. Jimmy tied the painter to the branch and let the boat hang down stream from the submerged tree.

The airboat would be coming out onto the main river about a mile away, and he would soon know whether it would be heading upstream away from him or downstream towards him.

Jim and Jenny Thompson waited in silence, both worried that Jimmy hadn't yet returned from fishing. Jenny recalled his promise; "I'll be home before dark." Jimmy usually kept his promises. Oh, he would sometimes argue with her requests saying, "You worry too much," but when she held firm he would honor her wishes. She knew he loved to fish and would often get caught up in the excitement of the moment; a good strike from a hefty bass would always take his mind off of getting home on time. Sometimes his little motor would fail and he would have to resort to the oars, which weren't quite as fast as the motor, but infinitely more reliable.

Jimmy was a carbon copy of his father and she loved him as much as she had loved her son. She and Jim hadn't lived on the river when they were raising Jimmy's father, Jason, but he had found plenty of ways to worry his mother and she recalled most of them still.

"Wha'do ya think Jenny?" Jim Thompson, (Jimmy's namesake) asked his wife. "It's getting dark."

"He promised me he would be back before dark." She had been listening for his little motor to come putt, putting around the bend. She and Jimmy had gone through this before. She thought she had him convinced that the river was too dangerous for a lone fisherman, at night in an unlighted boat, especially in the early spring when the big gators were so active. Just falling out of the boat and thrashing around to get back in could end in disaster for the boater and dinner for the gator. The gators, mostly inactive during the day, hunted at night. The biggest danger was not really gators but the boaters who had waited a little too late to start for home and were scurrying with their big motors, going too fast for the river. The airboats were the most dangerous; with no keel they had less control, especially in the turns. She had seen them slip sideways after entering a turn too fast. It would be hard

4

for them to avoid a boy in a small boat, if they saw him too late. Jimmy was good on the river, he used good sense, more than some kids his age, but she was sure he hadn't taken a flashlight to warn an oncoming boat driver of his presence after dark. "Let's give him a little while longer."

Jimmy heard the airboat as it turned onto the main river, it came his way fast, the distant thunder growing in volume. *Looks like the fishin's over for the day*, he thought. The airboat roared around the upstream bend and bore down on the tree where Jimmy had his boat tied off; he knew that if the idiot didn't slow way down there would be a big wake. He reached down quickly and pulled the stringer of fish into the boat, to prevent tangling in the submerged tree limbs, with the rocking of the boat. Jimmy stood in the tiny boat with his hand on the tree branch to keep his balance. He realized too late how strong the wave action would be. The airboat banked into a hard right turn then suddenly spun on its own axis, throwing a blast of wind from its prop and debris from the fallen tree right into Jimmy's face. His boat lurched as it took the huge wave over the gunnels. Jimmy lost his balance, fell out, and crashed hard against the fallen tree trunk. He fought to the surface, grabbed the side of his little boat, and then realized it was filling with water. His little boat had no flotation, and though made of wood, the weight of the outboard motor, the anchor, his trolling motor and the large gel-cell battery was more than it could support.

The airboat, having spun around 180 degrees, was once again upstream when the driver cut the engine, letting it slowly drift backwards towards the same tree that Jimmy's boat was tied to. The airboater's open mouthed, vacant expression went unnoticed by Jimmy as he scrambled into his sinking boat and frantically tried to gather his gear. His left wrist throbbed and his watch band felt loose. Losing the watch, one of his most cherished possessions, and collecting his fishing gear quickly faded from his immediate concerns. With water already rushing over the transom, he knew that baling would be a waste of time. He reached for a limb of the dead tree, but missed it as the boat slowly sank beneath him. Panic set in; something held his foot, pulling him under with the boat. He had his life preserver on, and being a good swimmer he didn't fear the water, but this was different.

"Help!" he screamed at the airboater, who stared expressionless, a few feet away, his boat resting now against the same branch Jimmy's boat remained tied to. "I'm caught," Jimmy yelled, and the boat continued to pull at his foot, the water at his chest and rising. He ducked under and struggled to release his foot, but the buoyancy of the life jacket pulling upward kept him from reaching it. Panic and the natural urge to fight for the surface, prevented him from discarding the false security of his life jacket, prevented him from ducking under, and trying again without it. The unsnapped hook on his stringer had caught in the shoelaces of his right foot, transforming his shoe into an unseen hand pulling him relentlessly into the depths of the river.

He screamed at the man, who only stared with unseeing eyes. "Help me, damn it, help me! I'm caught!" fear and anger thick in his powerful words, but the man on the airboat seemed to be in a stupor, the sound of Jimmy's voice bounced off his yellow earmuffs. Jimmy's life jacket helped him hold his head above water, but the boat rapidly sank deeper, the unseen hand pulling from below. He struggled in a futile effort to reach a branch of the tree. Choking now, his shouts no more than a series of coughs, fear consuming him with each choking swallow of water. He struggled to keep his head above the surface, his arms flailing, reaching upward in desperation, when a hand grasped his left wrist. The two wrists locked with an instant of hope. He and the airboater, fought against the weight of the boat, pulling him persistently under.

The pull of the boat seemed irresistible. He grew weak from his struggles and couldn't get a good breath of air without sucking in river water. His grip loosened on the airboater's wrist, his eyes wide with fright, returned the airboater's hopeless stare through the tannin stained water. He held his strangled breath against the desperate urge, to suck in with his lungs, his panic stricken mind telling him it would be alright, yet knowing better. In the few seconds before his consciousness left him and his grip on the airboater's arm relaxed completely, he felt a strange peace as segments of his life's memories drifted from his brain into blackness. Those final seconds, at deaths door, passed in slow motion as he surrendered his life with the image of his anguished grandmother, waiting for him in the darkness.

Jimmy couldn't feel his treasured watch slip off his injured wrist as his lifeless arm slipped through the airboater's grasp. He didn't hear the airboat motor start and drone off back upriver. He didn't feel the bass on his stringer struggling to free themselves, and in doing so free his foot from the open stringer snap that had caught in his shoelaces. He didn't feel the life jacket, which had worked against him earlier, float his lifeless body to the surface. He did not know of coming to rest around the bend, in the very shallows where he had hoped to cast his lures. He could not be grateful, for the hands that would later lift him from the water, too late.

"Jim, I think somethin's wrong. He should be home by now. It's pitch dark."

"Yeah, he's probably out of gas. I bet he went up to the second flats and thought he could drift back down before dark. He's probably a mile upstream now wishin' he hadn't been so ambitious."

Jenny said, "Let's go see if we can find him. I know he went upriver."

"I'll get the Whaler ready while you put our gear back in the shed," Jim said. "Why don't you bring the small gas can so I won't have to tow him back if he's out of gas?" Jim stepped off the dock into their Boston Whaler. He was pretty sure Jimmy wasn't out of gas and he and Jimmy had just tuned up the little motor with a new spark plug and carburetor adjustment. Sending her for the gas can was Jim's way of alleviating Jenny's fears, letting her believe it was something simple like being out of gas, but that didn't help him. He was worried himself. There was no moon tonight and it was pitch black. Jimmy would be hard to see from a fast moving boat, but there wasn't any traffic on the river. They hadn't heard a single boat and they had been on their dock for at least an hour before dark.

They heard the sound of a motor as they were getting their boat ready and putting away their fishing gear. They soon recognized it as an airboat, not Jimmy's little fishing skiff. The airboater passed in the main river with his searchlight sending shafts of light through the cypress trees towards their dock on the side channel. They couldn't see him or his boat through the dense forest, even with the trees winter bare. This was one of the attractions of their property; they had a good, deep hole right off their dock and a private, natural channel around an island, restricted at the upper end with a fallen tree. This prevented the river traffic from taking their channel as a short cut.

"That's one of the few gentlemen airboaters on the river," Jenny remarked, "He's goin' slow enough to spot another boater before it's too late."

"More'n likely it's someone who don't know the river," said Jim with a touch of sarcasm staining his words. "Let's go see if Jimmy needs some help."

Jim started the motor and searched quickly upstream, past Blue Spring with no sign of Jimmy or his boat. Their boat, as small as it was, couldn't explore the many side channels and sloughs, the shallow water and overhanging branches blocked their way, but they poked in as far as they could, calling out his name. They soon reached the flats where the river spread out a mile wide, a river of grass dotted with small hammocks and webbed with small channels. They didn't think he would have come this far up the river. They started back downstream, working more slowly after they passed Blue Spring, drifting with the current, quietly listening then calling out. Just past the submerged tree they spotted some assorted fishing gear, bobbers and floating lures caught up in the cypress roots in an outside bend of the river. Jim thought he recognized some of it as Jimmy's gear. He realized too late that his expression had told Jenny his thoughts when he saw her draw a deep breath.

"Oh Jim," Jenny pleaded, with tears wetting her cheeks, "what could have happened?"

Jim answered, "Don't jump to conclusions. He could have dropped his tackle box overboard. Maybe that's why he's late—tryin' to collect his gear?" His mind tried to dodge the seriousness of their discovery but the reality of it hammered his brain. He knew something bad had happened. *What?* Whatever had happened had happened upstream from here. Jim knew he had to do something and do it quick. Jenny was distraught and he wasn't far behind her. Jim throttled the ancient motor to the max and headed downriver.

"What's goin' on, Jim? We can't stop now, we have to find him."

"I'm goin' after Captain Mike," he said with a tight jaw. He saw the fear in Jenny's eyes and knew her heart was pounding as fast as his. *Mike would know where to look,* he thought to himself.

Chapter Two (Five years later)

From the sands of time

Jack Wade leveled off near the bottom, under thirty feet of cold clear water, and hung there looking at the wondrous beauty of Blue Spring. What passed as the bottom was really just where it narrowed, an opening too small for a man to pass through. As with most of these springs, the crystalline water found it's way out of the aquifer and into the Florida sunshine by rushing out of a fissure in the limestone, which merely marked the beginning, or end of a cave system, some large enough to boggle the mind. Some of the larger springs exit through openings, big enough to allow divers to enter and explore thousands of feet into the cave system, sometimes never reaching any limitation except their own. These underwater labyrinths claim diver's lives nearly every year. Blue Spring holds no such danger, that is except the normal dangers of man in an element that he was not designed to live in. Blue Spring had no overhanging rocks nor passages big enough for a diver to explore, just pure crystal water with white, sugar sand drifting ever downward towards the open fissure in the limestone bottom. Jack, an ex-Navy diver, loved to don his diving gear and explore the depths of the spring, occasionally bringing up some ancient artifact, a sliver of pottery or a discarded arrowhead.

Hanging suspended, one hand clutching a cleft in the limestone, the upward flow of the current stood him on his head. Jack's other hand, searching the soft, restless sand, near the edge of the final drop-off, struck something just beneath the surface. He knew that most objects thrown or dropped into the spring migrated towards the main opening over time. This was a diver's watch. It was not the first piece of jewelry he had found. These kids come here to swim, and get so anxious to be the first in their group to swing out on the big rope swing tied thirty feet up in the old cypress tree, that they forget to take their valuables out of their cutoffs or their watches and bracelets off their arms. Jack had to admit the swing was fun. He did it himself once in a while. Some of these kids would turn somersaults after releasing the rope. He longed to be young enough to try something like that once more, but he was afraid he would make a fool of himself.

He examined the watch, and could see it wasn't running. This was no kid's watch, it had a bezel with which to show elapsed time—an expensive version of the watch he wore himself. A Rolex diver's watch could be worth several thousand dollars. He would give it to John Trentwood, the president of the Arrowhead Development, Owner's Association. John knew every family in the area, and if he could identify who it belonged to, John would see that it got back to its rightful owner. He stuck it in his net sack and continued his dive.

Jack pulled the last few reluctant breaths from his tank in thirty feet of water, so clear it was like looking through air. He could see his wife standing at the water's edge a hundred feet away. He came up slowly, his tank supplying him with expanding air as the pressure decreased. A lot more tired than he felt he should be, he said to his wife, Martha, "Ain't as young as I used to be."

"You never were," his wife quipped. Her dry sense of humor had kept him chuckling inside, for close to forty years.

"I guess there's some truth to that," Jack smiled. "However, this old fart got a good haul today," he exclaimed as he held up the net. He dried off, opened a beer and sat down on the edge of the spring to examine his finds. He picked up the watch first and held it out for Martha to see. "Ain't that a beauty?"

Two days later Jack knocked on John Trentwood's door. "Hello," he said as John opened the door."

"Hi, Jack, It's good to see you."

"Thanks, John. I brought that watch I told you I found."

"Yeah," John said, "I don't know who it could belong to. There hasn't been anything reported lost for some time now. Nobody swims in Blue Spring till summer . . . too cold for 'em."

11

"That's just one of the mysteries of life John. Blue Spring is the same temperature year round. If you can stand 72 degrees in the summer, you can stand it in the winter."

"I can hardly stand it in the summer, Jack. But it *is* mighty refreshin' if you got the hot summer sun to warm you up afterwards."

"Yeah, you need a wet suit though, even in summer, if you stay down very long, specially when your as old as I am, and been livin' in Florida half your life. As they say, 'My blood's too thin.' Them Canadians come down here in December and think nothin' of swimmin' off the beach when the Gulf temperature is down in the seventies just like Blue Spring."

"I'd freeze my ass off," laughed John. He took the watch from Jack and whistled softly, "I bet that baby cost a pretty penny. I've heard about the Rolex watches, but I never saw one before."

"Yeah this one may be ruined, it's not working and it's full of water. Looks a little dark on the inside, like it's been underwater a long time. Whoever owns it may have insurance on it, or it might have some sentimental value. There's no engravin' on it, just some numbers. You can take it to the next meeting and ask around a bit. If nobody claims it, I'd like to have it back." Jack turned to go and said, "I may make the meetin' myself but I thought you would be there for sure. Anyway, I'll catch you later, John. Give my best to the Missus."

"So long, Jack."

Chapter Three

Who will take the responsibility?

Captain Mike Tracy reached for the net. The act of picking up another's trash had become a habit, unwilling at first, then compulsive, but never failing to bolster Mike's hatred for the one who left it. He lumped them all into one big category called assholes. This category held all discourteous boat and automobile drivers, pushy people and a few others. He had no use for those who would defile the environment in which they lived. *No animal fouls its own nest.* He would curse them out loud when alone, or mumble his obscenities under his breath when he had customers aboard. It was doubly degrading to have to pick up someone else's trash, and have to do it in front of others. It was as if the human race had let him down and he was ashamed for them. He had grown to accept it as his duty and to call as little attention to it as possible. But his silence hid his growing frustration, the frustration born from the realization that few of his customers really cared.

A person might think that Mike tried to keep the river clean to impress his customers, but they would be wrong. He would pick up the empty beer can or discarded bait box, even when alone, and would act the same if he didn't have his Lazy River Tours. He loved the river, lived for the river and in doing so, passed on his love for the river to his customers, in varying degrees, according to their ability to open their minds to his philosophy. He ran two pontoon boats at different times, one for sightseeing tours of various lengths and one for guided fishing trips.

The airboats drove him up a wall. He could scarcely contain his emotions when one came charging around the bend, even

13

if the driver was thoughtful enough to slow down. The driver, no matter how courteous, was automatically thrown into Mike's asshole category by just the fact that he operated such a heinous machine. These machines defiled the river, mocked the river, and transformed the river into a wild, noisy, unfriendly place, fit only for machines. He had determined that it wasn't the speed that offended him so much as the noise. Their deep thunderous vibrations could be felt, as well as heard, well over a mile away, increasing in volume until the cacophony of straight exhaust pipes screamed their arrival. It was never a surprise when one approached, no matter how suddenly it appeared through the cypress boughs. He began to measure the quality of each day on the river, by whether or not he encountered an airboat, and by how many he did encounter, instead of how much money he did or did not make.

Some times his thoughts would turn to ways to get them off the river. These thoughts only added to his overall frustration with the assholes in his life. If he brought up the subject with someone from the area, he would meet with one of three attitudes: the same hatred he felt in different degrees, a complicity born of ignorance, or a "so what?" attitude. He could understand the hatred angle, and he loved to educate the ignorant, but for some knowing person to condone such machines led him to the opinion that the person he was talking to was about to join his select group. In the company of an ally, the beer talk would sometime lead to easy ways to rid the river of airboats. These quick remedies were designed to be humorous, and some of them caused him to have more than a chuckle. Like the time Bernie suggested a rifle loaded with tranquilizer darts. Shoot the driver in the ass and watch him glide off into the swamp. And some, were mentioned in a less serious manner than the results would bring. Bernie wanted to string a cable that could be lowered at the right time. Someone suggested a little plastic explosive in the right place, sugar in the gas tank, etc.

Numerous hair-brained schemes usually floated around in his gray matter, all of them frustrating, in that they were all on the outer fringes of his philosophy of respecting the rights of others, as well as being illegal. He did recognize, that forcing his will on another group would put him square on his own select list, as far as that group was concerned. It was equally frustrating to talk to someone like John Wood, who agreed with him about the nuisance value of the airboats but would approach the problem from a political standpoint. John would say, "Those things have been around forever. They are firmly entrenched in the heritage of the area. Right or wrong, it would be hard to get legislation against them." Mike was not of that world anyway. He was not political. He met his problems directly without compromise, never beating around the bush. He neither asked for, nor needed, the support of others. He felt helpless and restricted in his private war against airboats. He felt that a solution would come to him someday, and when it did he would surely live up to the task of implementing it. His new friend, Al Banner felt the same way, and Mike thought Al would come up with something, although it was apt to be more conventional than Mike's ideas. Al, a lawyer, expressed confidence that he could come up with something that would at least quieten them down.

Mike deposited the empty beer can in the trash container and pushed the throttle forward, his last run of the day was nearly over. He turned the wheel upriver, towards Stumpknockers, a restaurant and bar named after the Florida equivalent to small pan-fish. He kept his 24 ft. Pontoon boat docked there for his river tours. They called it Stumpys for short and the specialty of the house was fried or blackened catfish, which people would drive all the way from Ocala to wait in line for. He was meeting Al and his wife Sarah for a couple of beers and a plate full of the best catfish in Florida.

Al and Sarah had just bought a home on the river, after taking one of Mike's tours and falling in love with the river and the area. Mike liked them both and appreciated the attention they bestowed on him. Mike was anxious to talk to Al this evening. Al had left a cryptic message on his machine, indicating that something was up in the association, and knew Mike would be interested. Mike goosed the throttle a little more than usual, cutting his downriver trip a little short, time-wise. He deposited his group of passengers, closing his ears to the grumbles about time, and walked through the parking lot towards the bar where Al and Sarah waited.

Chapter Four

The Awakening

Al and Sarah Banner waited for Mike at the bar, they were having a drink and discussing Mike and wondering between them how he would take this. "Perhaps we should not have volunteered to pass this chore on to Mike?" asked Sarah. She had told Al long ago the story of Jimmy Thompson, which others had pieced together for her, one by one. Mike had never talked about it to either one of them. She told Al that she thought Mike had taken it as hard as the Thompsons. She said, "This may be hard for Mike to accept if the watch really did belong to Jimmy."

"He's a big boy," said Al, "I think he can handle it. Besides, we're committed and here he comes now."

Mike entered the bar at Stumpknockers, kissed Sarah on the cheek and shook Al's hand saying, "Where's my beer?"

"Coming up partner," said Al. "I ordered when I saw you pull into your slip."

"You have some catching up to do," said Sarah, holding up her nearly finished drink.

"I can handle that," Mike replied. "What's up with the association?"

"Well, if you would attend the meetings you would know," suggested Al.

"You know I can't handle that crap," Mike said in mock anger. His mind flashed back to the time he nearly decked his neighbor at one of the meetings because he didn't agree with what the man wanted to do about the road. The neighbor was wrong but could express himself more fluently, and he seemed to have the crowd going his way. Quieting his opposition one way or another, seemed the only solution to Mike at the time. Jim Thompson,

16

sitting next to him, saw it coming and calmed him down before it came to blows. Mike hadn't attended a meeting since. Mike knew that Al had heard that story and was just needling him.

Mike thought he and Al were alike in a lot of ways but that Al had a knack for controlling his anger to a more efficient end. Mike felt more in control of his anger since he started the river tours, an environment, where he was always in charge. He collected his money up front and would take no shit off an unruly guest. Mike, at a lanky six feet, wasn't physically imposing, But he possessed a demeanor or aura that usually prevented, even larger men from challenging his demands, and he never hesitated to use it. He knew that stories like that, and the one about Brier's Point, circulated all around him. He recalled the big guy, who had had a little too much to drink and wouldn't shut up, kept trying to make a joke out of everything he said. He remembered the guy's defiant look when he finally stopped the boat at Brier's Point and asked him to step ashore. The passenger refused, saying, "I don't want to fight you." Mike went up to him, grabbed his arm with a submissive judo hold and marched him to the front of the boat and off onto shore. Mike proceeded to back the boat away from Brier's Point saying loud enough to drown out the big guy's cussing, "I'll give your wife directions to pick you up." Evidently his wife who was aboard had no objections to Mike's action. Mike never knew if she did indeed pick him up.

"Mike, I got a feeling you can handle anything if you put your mind to it," Al commented, "but just drink your beer and listen. The meeting was called to discuss the pros and cons of airboats on the Withlacoochee River, and you should have been there, since you have more direct knowledge of how it affects the river than anyone I know. However, one item which was not on the agenda came up that you should be aware of. Jack Wade is a local air boater and scuba diver. He is elderly and usually dives in Blue Spring for artifacts."

"I know Jack," interrupted Mike. "He is one of the few truly courteous drivers on the river."

"Yes, so I've heard," said Al. "It's not uncommon for Jack to find a wallet or some piece of jewelry at the spring, then turn it over to John Trentwood to find the owner. Well, last weekend he found a watch. It appeared to be a very expensive, very good diver's watch. It had a minute crack in the crystal and was not running. It was full of water, but Jack thought it might have some value to the owner—in insurance money, or it could perhaps be repaired—so he gave it to John. John's eighteen year old son was at the meeting, and made the comment that Jimmy Thompson, who had drowned in the river a few years ago, had had a watch just like that."

Mike's hair started up on the back of his neck.

Al hesitated before continuing, "John said he knew the Thompsons and knew how hard the boy's death had been on the grandparents. He had heard they grieved so hard, they almost sold their place on the river, it held such painful memories. Never one to do something he could get someone else to do, John asked if anyone knew them well enough to show them the watch, to see if it was Jimmy's. I commented that I knew you lived next to them, and was very close to both Jenny and Jim Thompson, and that I would ask you to present the watch to them, and he agreed to it." As Al said this, he reached in his pocket and handed the watch to Mike.

Mike was speechless as he stared at the watch in silent reverence. Jimmy's grandma had given it to him after his father's death. His father was an avid diver and spared no expense on his equipment. Jimmy was proud of the watch and rarely took it off. The fact that it had turned up in Blue Spring was a mystery. Maybe the kid had lost it there and was afraid to tell his grandma. No, that didn't make sense. Jimmy would have exhausted every possibility of finding the watch at the time it was lost, which would have included him asking me to help, thought Mike. He would have asked me to dive with him in the spring to find it— Jimmy wasn't certified but he dove the spring several times, him snorkeling and me with my tank, once in a while buddy breathing with him so he could extend his underwater time to get to the bottom of the spring. Jimmy would have made a good diver.

How could he show this to Jenny? It would break her heart all over again. He knew she and Jim hadn't forgotten, and that they still thought of Jimmy every day. He often thought of him himself. They had some great times together, he and Jim, Jenny and Jimmy. Could he bring this all back to the present? *He knew he had to.* There was no one else. No one else could ease the shock to the Thompsons, as he knew he had to.

"It's his watch," he said, with constricted throat. "I'll take it to them."

Al and Sarah, seemed to sense his anguish, and waited silently while he gathered his emotions in order to speak. It was as if they could feel his pain, as the old memories tormented him.

Mike pocketed the watch without a word. He took a long pull at the beer, sat it down and said, "Please excuse me. I have to go. I'll call you tomorrow." His mind was whirling as he sat the half beer down, hugged Sarah limply, gave a halfhearted wave to Al, turned and walked toward his pickup truck. His mind didn't even register their closing goodbyes. He had to think and think quick.

As he drove home he reflected on the last few days of Jimmy's life. When was the last time he had seen the watch? How did it get in the spring? Did Jimmy fall, crack the crystal, and then throw it in the spring in disgust? No, he was smart enough to know the value of the watch and knew that it could have been repaired. He wouldn't have lost it swimming in the spring, it was too cold when you got out that time of year—unless it was on a dare from some other kid. I would have heard about that. Why was the crystal cracked? When had the watch stopped running, at the same time the crystal cracked or when it simply ran out of juice? There weren't any rocks in the spring to crack the crystal, except way down deep. Jenny would know if he lost the watch; he knew Jimmy would sometimes tell her things he wouldn't tell him or Jim. He had to get some answers. He wondered exactly where Jack found it. He would ask him now, if he could get him on the phone. He headed for the payphone at the corner while his mind swept him back in time to that horrible night he would never forget, the knock on the door that signaled a drastic change in his life and the lives of his next door neighbors, leaving them devastated for the second time in two years.

Chapter Five (Five years ago)

Worried

Mike's pleasant trip down the Withlacoochee was suddenly interrupted by a knock in his new outboard motor. He eased the throttle but the knock persisted. He tried to shut the motor down but the knock persisted even louder. His senses kicked in as his mind approached wakefulness and his neighbor's voice joined the knocking. He jumped up from the couch where he had fallen asleep and opened the door. He knew something was wrong before any words came from his next door neighbor's mouth. Jim Thompson was not an excitable person, never prone to panic, but he saw panic in Jim's eyes, and heard it in his voice.

Jim said, with bated breath, "Something's happened to Jimmy. Can you help us look for him?"

Mike reached for his jacket to ward off the night chill and said "Sure, Jim." He hurried through the door and put his hand on Jim's shoulder, "Don't worry we'll find him."

On the way to the Thompson's boat dock, Jim pulled Mike behind the big live oak tree, out of Jenny's sight as she waited in the Whaler. "Mike I don't want to alarm Jenny unnecessarily, but I can tell you. We found some fishing gear, bobbers, a couple of lures and such, hung up in the cypress roots just below the shallows, down from where that big cypress fell across the river last fall. I think it's Jimmy's stuff. *Oh Lord Mike,* I think somethin's happened to Jimmy. We searched quick all the way up to the second flats and saw this stuff on the way back. We couldn't get into some of the sloughs with the brush and all, but we hollered our lungs out. Jimmy would have answered us if he was back up in one of them sloughs. Wha'do ya think?"

"Slow down, Jim. We'll find him. I'll tie my kayak behind the Whaler so I can search the sloughs. Jimmy may just be stranded somewhere and didn't hear you holler."

They started their search below the shallows and probed the black, moonless night with flashlights. Eerie shadows from the cypress knees danced on the adjoining tree trunks, casting a ghostly atmosphere over their search. The twin dots of gator eyes reflected back to remind them of the dangers this river held at night. The three of them searched and hollered.

Exhausted and exasperated with the futility of their efforts, they woke one of their neighbors up the river. "Hey, George, its Mike, Mike Tracy. I hate to bother you this time of night but we got an emergency here. Can I use your phone?"

"Sure, Cap'n Mike. Come on in. What's the trouble? Is there anything I can do?"

Mike told him about Jimmy being missing while they walked to the phone, then asked him, "George, did you see Jimmy this afternoon?" Mike asked.

"Why yes, as a matter of fact, I did. It was well before dark though. He was in that little gray skiff: he was headin' down river. I was sittin' in the kitchen and saw him through the window."

"Well he never made it home. We found some of his fishing gear caught up under some cypress knees a couple of miles downstream."

"My Lord, Mike! I'll get my coat while you call the sheriff. And I'll get the missus to make us some coffee. You look like you could use it."

"Thanks, George, any help would be appreciated, and the coffee would hit the spot." Mike got a quick answer and explained the situation to the dispatcher. She asked for his name, the address, and phone number then said she would have a deputy call him right back.

"Please miss this can't wait. It's not just the case of a teenager that's staying out too late; this river is dangerous at night. Can you send someone over to help us search? "

"Yes Sir. I'm dialing the substation as we speak. If you hang up someone will call you right back."

Mike hung up and sat down by the phone with his head in his hands. He knew they wouldn't treat this as urgent unless he could convince someone how serious it was. He heard George's wife, Martha, fussing with the coffee pot in the kitchen. He sure needed a cup of coffee.

Four minutes later the phone rang and Mike answered it.

"This is Deputy Buck Stone. What's the trouble, Mike?"

A wave of relief swept over Mike. He knew Buck Stone and knew he was talking to the right person. Two minutes later he hung up the phone and smelled the coffee. Martha had fixed a big pot and filled a thermos which she handed to him along with three cups. He thanked her and went out to the Thompsons. George came out right behind him and went straight to his boat and started the engine.

"I guess we'll keep lookin' till the sheriff gets here," George said, and Mike gave him a solemn nod.

————————

There were no other houses right on the river for several miles. The thick Florida woods, bordered with cypress along the river, widened to swamps in places, with numerous sloughs leaving, then rejoining the river downstream. It was slow going, with Mike probing the sloughs in his kayak while Jim and Jenny yelled till they were hoarse. George worked one side of the river in his john boat, while Jim and Jenny worked the other. Mike could see the despair clouding Jim and Jenny's faces and fought to keep his own fears hidden from them. Between yells, Jim and Jenny couldn't talk, except to point out something, or whisper a new theory from throats tightened with fear and guilt. This guilt would deepen in the days, months and years that followed.

Chapter Six

Reality sets in

Deputy Sheriff Buck Stone, out of the Hernando substation and one of his officers joined the search later that night. Official searches for a missing teenager will not usually take place that quickly. The police know that nine times out of ten, or maybe ninety-nine times out of a hundred the teenager will wander in the next day with some cock and bull story, or a, "I told you I was going to spend the night with Buster." But Buck knew both Jim Thompson and Mike Tracy and knew this was real.

Buck at a solid six foot three, was a commanding figure. His nearly sixty years of age had left him still ramrod straight with the serious vigor of a younger man. He had been more than a deputy a few years back. He was the head honcho, the high sheriff of Citrus county. No one thought he would ever lose his job, that is until his wife died and he couldn't handle the grief. His normal workaholic habits fell by the wayside. He was given to long periods of depression, where he just didn't seem to give a damn. He lost the election that year to his right hand man, Bill Conway, who only ran because he knew Buck just couldn't handle it anymore. Some folks say that Buck even voted for Bill Conway, but that would have been out of character for Buck; he would have had more respect for the folks that supported him in the election. Buck wouldn't even have run for office that year, if some of his long time constituents hadn't railroaded him into it. Bill hired Buck as a deputy the following year. Bill had seen that Buck needed something in his life to pull him out of the past and knew he was still a good cop. His responsibility to his job soon took over and it was then that Buck started his return to the real world, leaving his grief behind. Buck ran the tiny substation in Hernando, and though he never aspired to anything grander, people still thought of Buck as Sheriff. Those who knew him still called him sheriff, and those who met him for the first time thought of him as a sheriff. His age, the way he carried himself, and the white Stetson, all these gave the impression of sheriff, and Buck didn't discourage it. Bill Conway gave him a free hand in doing his job, and he had a regretful one ahead of him now.

They used the neighbor's house as a rest spot and a place to vent new theories, refreshing their caffeine loaded brains with more coffee throughout the night. At daybreak the following morning, Mike and Jim found Jimmy's empty swamped boat, still tied to the tree, sunken out of view from their probing flashlights, the well worn painter tied low on a branch, the only connection between Jimmy's world as it used to be and the darkness below the surface.

Chapter Seven

The search for knowledge

The next day brought reinforcements. While the Thompsons looked on, with defeated hopelessness, Buck and the deputies dragged the river. This was no mean feat with all the sunken trees and rocks to get snagged on. The boy's boat held no clues as to what had happened. It had no sign of a collision, the stringer, with three nice bass and one open snap, was still attached to the transom of the boat.

Buck Stone poured over his thoughts in his slow methodical fashion . . . It's peculiar we never found his life jacket, he thought, his grandma said he definitely had with him. If it was just laying in the boat and floated away, we would find it. If he had it on, we would find him, even if a gator found him first. A gator can't eat much at one setting. They return to a kill several times. The bright yellow life jacket would have floated him, or maybe what was left of him, and the gator damn sure wouldn't eat the life jacket. If he fell from the boat, hit his head and knocked himself unconscious, would he have drowned? What sunk the boat? It hadn't turned over. Maybe the boy had fallen overboard and just swamped it trying to get back in? But that didn't cut it either. He could have walked out on the trunk of the fallen tree his boat was tied to. There wasn't any rational reason to suspect foul play, but things were not always what they seemed. It's hard to figure a gator into the occasion but we can't rule it out either. A big one could have gotten hold of him if he had fallen out of the boat, thrashing around trying to get back in. If that had happened, he could have swamped the boat while tussling with the gator. In that event the life preserver would have been no use to him. If a gator had him and wallowed him in the mud, the yellow life preserver would be hard to see even from the air.

Something bothered him and he couldn't figure what it was. He was certain the boy was dead, drowned and either washed downstream or dragged into the brush by a gator. The body could have washed up under the undercut banks and snagged on the clawing fingers of the cypress knees. These questions would nag the Buck from time to time, until he eventually found the grisly answer. Buck reckoned that if they didn't find him soon, the hardest part would be telling the grandparents that it was no use.

He had organized a search with volunteers along the river banks upstream and downstream a mile each way from where the boat was found. He had requisitioned a chopper in to run a search up and down the river, but even that gave no hope of finding the boy, or what was left of him. He sent divers down in the area where they found Jimmy's boat and they came up nearly empty handed. The divers found some of Jimmy's fishing gear, his good rod and reel, some small stuff that probably fell out as the boat angled under stern first, weighted by the motor on the transom. Most of the things the diver came up with had not been under long. A few things like an old trolling motor had been there for years he thought. A pair of bright yellow, aviator style earmuffs, which some air-boater had dropped, was found about a quarter mile downstream.

He hoped the grandparents didn't press him for answers cause he didn't have any. He'd ask around and try to find out if anyone saw Jimmy on the river and if so what time. He wondered if the boy had been up to the spring? It was too chilly to swim but he could have been fishing at the spring. Maybe John Trentwood would know or at least be able to tell him who might have been there. John, the association president knew just about everyone in the development. The homes were widely scattered as most of the residents liked their privacy and there were very few homes right on the river downstream from the spring. It was highly unlikely that anyone saw or heard anything that evening but he would ask around.

He called John Trentwood, who told him, "Charlie Curtis sometimes goes to the spring on nice days, even if the weather's cold. I think he was there that day."

Buck finally got around to questioning Charlie. "Yeah, sheriff, I was there but there weren't any kids there," said Charlie. "We drove up in the car, cause it was a little chilly on the river, and had some hamburgers on the grill. We left just before dark and we were the last ones to leave. Orin and Betty Taylor were at the spring that day." Charlie hesitated, then said, "Orin left just before we did."

"Who's we, Charlie," the Buck asked, waited for an answer then said, "Who was with you?"

"Oh! . . . Just the wife and the kids."

"Did you know Jimmy?"

"No, I knew of him and seen him on the river fishin', but I never met him. I knew he stayed with his grandparents after his parents got killed. I bet they're takin' this hard."

"Yeah, they are; they can't hardly answer my questions without chokin' up." Buck felt he had gotten all he needed from Charlie and started towards his car. "Well Charlie, If you hear anything that might help us figure out what happened, let me know," Buck said and slipped him his card.

Charlie said. "I thought the kid just fell in and drowned."

Buck recognized it as a question and replied in his matter of fact way, "That is the case Charlie, as far as we know. We're just askin' around to piece together the entire story. We don't have anything to indicate that it's any more complicated than that. Just let us know if you hear anything."

"OK, sheriff, will do," Charlie said.

Orin Taylor swayed, his whiskey breath drifting through the screen, as Buck Stone stood outside his door the next day. Buck, seeing he would not be invited in, asked him about being at the spring on the day the boy drowned and Orin said he was, and asked him what he could do for him.

"Were you by yourself?" remembering that Charlie had said Orin's wife Betty was there also.

"My wife Betty was there."

"I understand you left just before dark. Did you see the boy at the spring or on your way home?" Buck asked.

"No sir, it got dark quick and I had to slow way down and use the light all the way home." he said in a slow and deliberate manner. "I would have seen him for sure if he had been fishin' that section of the river."

"What time did you leave the spring, Orin?"

"I don't rightly know sheriff, at least not exactly; it was just getting' dark. But, come to think of it, I did see someone comin' down river as I was leaving the spring, but they was too far away to tell who they was. They was just comin' around that bend way up river."

"What kind of boat was it, Orin? Was it a fishin' skiff?

"I think so," said Orin.

"What color was it?" asked Buck. He was getting interested now.

"I don't know," said Orin. "It was pretty dark and he was a long way off."

"It was a he?" asked Buck.

"Oh!" exclaimed Orin, "Uh . . . I don't know. I guess I just assumed it was a he. I couldn't see that far."

Buck paused and looked hard at Orin.

"Was this person alone in the boat?"

"I think so." said Orin. "But I'm not sure."

"Did your wife see this boat too?"

"No."

He had a feeling he was either being lied to or not being told something. Buck thought about what had just been said and decided to give Orin some time to hang himself. Changing direction, he asked, "Were you in a hurry? Didn't you want to get home before dark?

"Dark on this river don't scare me."

"Was you goin' fast?"

"No, I was goin' real slow—had my light on too—cause it was real dark out that night, there was no moon."

This jived with the Thompsons story which only put one airboat on the river in the right time frame and it was moving slow with its light on. That had to be Orin.

"Why didn't your wife see the fishing boat, Mr. Taylor?"

"She wasn't there." said Orin.

"But you said she was with you."

Orin started to act intimidated; his speech became less deliberate, more spontaneous, "Betty *was* there at the spring, but she didn't ride home with me."

Buck remembered that Charlie said Orin was there and left just before dark, but hadn't mentioned that Orin's wife hadn't ridden away with him on the airboat. *Why the hell wouldn't she ride home with him?* He thought.

"Why didn't she ride home with you?" asked Buck.

"Aw, she wasn't feeling good and Charlie Curtis offered to take her home." Orin said.

Buck thought it peculiar that Charlie hadn't mentioned taking the Taylor girl home. *Did Charlie have something to hide?* He didn't think so. Charlie's one of the good guys. He just hadn't thought it was important. "Where *is* your wife, Orin? I'd like to talk to her."

"I don't know, she was gone when I woke up this morning," Orin lied, which was a half-truth since she had been gone for the last two days.

"Well, Orin," said Buck, "let me know if you remember anything else after you sober up. You really should lay off the booze. It'll get you in trouble in the long run."

Orin stared at Buck, obviously angry that he would presume to preach to him from his own porch. He mumbled, "Yeah, yeah, yeah," as he started closing the door.

"Oh, by the way," Buck said, as he paused on the steps. "Ask your wife to call me soon." Buck felt a slight bit uncomfortable with Orin's answers, and it wouldn't hurt to get a second opinion.

"Yeah, sure," Orin said grudgingly, and closed the door with a harsh finality.

Chapter Eight (back to present)

Heartache

Jim heard Mike's 64 Chevy pickup pull in, and looked up from cleaning a few of the stump knockers he had caught fly-fishing, that afternoon. He released most of the fish he landed, but would keep a few plump ones for breakfast. He and Jenny loved to fry up the small boneless fillets and serve them with scrambled eggs and grits for breakfast. Both he and Jenny caught their share of bass out of the river too, but usually released them unless they were having someone over for a fish fry.

"How was your dinner?" Jim called out from his dock as Mike got out of the truck. Mike had told him earlier he was meeting the Banners at Stumpys for dinner.

"I didn't eat," Mike said, and before Jim could question him he said, "Where's Jenny, in the house?"

"Yeah, she's cooking dinner while I collect our breakfast for tomorrow morning," said Jim, with a grin.

"You got any beer in there? I need one," remarked Mike.

"We got your favorite cooled down and ready. Come on in," he said as he walked toward the house.

"We got company," he said to Jenny, "We're going to have a beer. Will you join us?"

She turned from the sink and smiled. "Of Course!" she exclaimed. "Just make yourself comfortable out there on the porch and I'll bring 'em to you." She wiped her hands and reached into the refrigerator.

Mike was glad to see she was coming right out. He only wanted to say what he had to say to both of them and didn't want to beat around the bush to either of them beforehand. As Jenny handed him his beer he said, "I got something to show you." He

30

had thought it over and decided the direct approach would be the best. It would be the words that followed the initial shock that meant the most. And with no more ado he laid the watch on the wicker table and said, "It wasn't found on Jimmy. It was found in Blue Spring." Giving them the idea that Jimmy's remains had been found would be a bad mistake. They had prayed to God to find the body but had lost hope of that long ago. No sense reviving that false hope now. The watch would do enough damage.

They both stared at the watch for a while and then Jim picked it up and examined it carefully, as if it held something inside, or would show him something they didn't want to know about, then said in a whisper, "Tell us more Mike." and reached out for Jenny with his right hand.

Mike knew they had seen the date on the watch, when Jenny gasped and put her hand to her mouth. Jim squeezed her hand to comfort her. Mike related the story he had just heard from Jack Wade, while he watched them. He could see the grief creep over their faces like a lace curtain. It veiled their eyes and misted them with yet to come tears as they slowly absorbed the possibilities this astounding discovery hinted of. Mike finished and waited for one of them to speak.

Jenny started to ask, "How....?" and choked up with a huge lump in her throat.

"How did it get there?" Mike said, and she nodded. "No one knows for sure, and I was trying to remember when I had seen it last," he offered, hoping she would be able to add something, then gained the strength to ask, "Wasn't that the date?"

"That was the date and Jimmy had it on the night he disappeared," Jim said with a faraway look in his eyes. "Jenny told him to be back before dark and he looked at his watch to see how much time that gave him. It was runnin' fine then."

"Do you think Jimmy could have lost it swimming in the spring?" Mike asked, but he already knew the answer.

"No," they both said at the same time.

"He only had a couple of hours to fish and I am sure that was all he had in mind," Jim went on to explain.

"He didn't have any trunks under his pants and I don't think he ever went in there in his birthday suit," Jenny offered, "especially not that time of year."

"Can we be sure it was his watch?" Mike asked.

"It's his," Jim said, "but we can check our papers and see if the serial number matches. His dad had it insured. It was worth a lot of money, you know. And when we gave it to Jimmy we thought about renewing the insurance when it came due, so we kept the paperwork. It was in with a whole bunch of other valuables. We just never got around to it."

"Truth is, we couldn't afford to," Jenny offered with a sad look in her eyes.

Mike knew they were on a fixed retirement income and thought there might be a lot of things they couldn't afford. Jim's son Jason had lived high on the hog and had expensive things but left Jim & Jenny with a financial burden when he and his wife lost their lives to a senseless accident on Highway 19. Jim had told him about the heavy mortgages on his son's home, fancy leased cars and especially the huge powerboat that ate up repair bills, slip fees and brokerage fees just to get it sold. They had gone through hell settling the estate and trying to hold out enough to get Jimmy into college. Jimmy was only about eleven years old at the time and Jason had not started to worry all that much about Jimmy's college tuition. Jim had always said that Jason was confident in his future earning ability and felt there would be no problem. Life's full of surprises. About half of them are unwelcome.

Mike looked at Jenny and said, "I know you don't want to open this up again, but we have to give this to the Sheriff. Maybe he can make some sense of it."

"I'm starting to make some sense of it myself," said Jim with a tight expression on his face.

Mike had that feeling in the back of his neck again, the one that started the hair to raise. He knew it would come to this. Jim wanted those same answers he had been searching for. They had answered a couple of them for him. He asked Jim & Jenny to see if they could find those papers and told them he would call the sheriff and tell him about the watch. He figured the sheriff would want to at least look at and verify the serial number. He may keep it for evidence if he determined there was foul play. Mike left Jim and Jenny on the porch and looked back when he was almost to his door. They hadn't moved. They were sitting there just looking at the watch in Jenny's hand.

Chapter Nine

If at first you don't succeed

Buck came over that night. Mike had asked him to see him before he talked to the Thompsons and it was about 8:30pm when he arrived. "Hey Buck, long time no see," said Mike as Sheriff Stone stepped onto the screened porch. "Sit down Buck, it's good to see you squeaked through another change of power after the election. I guess the new Sheriff doesn't have a friend who wants your job?"

"Aw," Buck said sheepishly, "they'll never get rid of me. Nobody wants to work hard enough to keep this job. Anyhow, what's up?"

Mike filled him in on the watch and gave him Jack Wade's phone number, asked him to take it easy on the Thompsons and Buck assured him he would. Then Mike got down to business. "Buck, I'm getting a strange feeling about Jimmy's disappearance," he volunteered, hoping for some support in this area. Buck just sat there leaving Mike hanging. "Come on Buck," he pleaded. "Give me some answers, or at least ideas."

"I don't have any answers for you, Mike. And I don't deal in ideas until I have a reason to. I'll go get the watch and verify it was Jimmy's and if it was I'll work from there."

"Jesus, Buck, don't you see what it means if Jimmy didn't lose the watch and was wearing it that night? Mike said with a little irritation showing in his voice.

"Sure Mike, I see what your getting' at, but first things first. No sense getting' all caught up in some fantasy until I get somethin I can sink my teeth into." These were the words he spoke but his mind was already on another track. Buck thought to himself, *Mike's a 'Let's get it done now' sort of guy, and he's on a fishing expedition to find out what I know*. Buck wasn't about to share his information with Mike, not that he had much to add except his own feelings. After all it had been five years. He still had a file on the case and would refresh his memory after his coffee in the morning, but there was something nagging him that he couldn't get a handle on.

"Christ Buck, can't you get your teeth into that watch?"

"Slow down Mike. Give me some breathin' room. You and me are on the same side. This case was always a mystery and we all want to solve it. Goin' off half cocked now ain't gonna to solve nothing. Consider the Thompsons. How do you think they're gonna feel if we get every body excited and it leads to nowhere?"

Mike, obviously suppressing a slight touch of anger at being talked to like a child, said in a calm, steady voice, "I'm sure you will try to figure this thing out, and I know those of us close to Jimmy will help you in any way we can, but I know there is an answer, and if it involves foul play, I want to know about it, and I know Jim and Jenny would too."

"Mike, this situation calls for a smooth, steady approach. The best thing you can do . . . is try to keep the Thompsons calm and not pump them full of false hopes. Now, just let me go to work," Buck said with a small touch of finality in his voice.

"I'm sorry," Mike apologized. "I guess I just got too excited. Thanks for coming here first."

"Its OK, Mike, believe me, I understand."

Buck went on over to the Thompsons and asked about the same questions that Mike had asked and got the same answers. He hated his job when he had to make people like the Thompsons dig back into such painful memories. He picked up the watch, put it in an envelope along with the insurance papers, and got Jim to sign a receipt while telling them he would verify the serial number. They asked him what finding the watch in Blue Spring meant and he gave them an evasive answer which seemed to satisfy them, but he knew that was only the result of their politeness and that in time he would have to come up with a better answer. He said his goodbyes and got behind the wheel when he suddenly remembered what had been eating at his sub-conscience after five years. He left and drove home with a renewed vigor.

He didn't sleep too well that night as old conversations crept through his mind. The watch brought a disturbing quality to an incident that heretofore had been considered an accident. He was as sure as Mike Tracy that the watch was an indicator of foul play. Had he missed something important in the first go round?

Chapter Ten

Delayed recall

Buck woke up the next day with his head buzzing. He had a full day ahead of him with a court appearance and a couple of warrants to serve. It was Gus's day off and Barb was stuck with holding the office down by herself most of the day. He wouldn't have time to do much research on the Thompson kid's case but he wanted to get the file and do some reading. He would have a little time at court while waiting to be called. He had arrived early and relieved Tommy who had had a rough night with a drunk down at the Crossroads bar. The drunk was snoring his head off in the back cell. By the time Barb came in he had a large pot of coffee brewing and had retrieved the file. He had gone straight to the thing which had been eating him the night before and wondered why he hadn't remembered it five years ago. It didn't seem important then and may not be important now but it sure as hell was what he called a loose end that needed to be tied.

His notes were a little loose. He didn't use a computer back then like some of his contemporaries. He relied on his hand written notes which he regimented himself to write at the earliest possible moment after questioning someone, even if it meant a short night's sleep. Now he gave them to Barb and she transcribed them into a computer for him. It sure cut down on the paperwork.

He went back to His conversation with Charlie Curtis. Charlie had said that Orin was at the spring and left before he did and that was just before dark. He hadn't said anything about giving Orin's wife (her name was Betty) a ride home. Yet that was what Orin had said. Why hadn't Charlie told him? Charlie figured it wasn't important was the only answer. He knew Charlie well enough to think he wouldn't hide something on purpose. But Buck had been around long enough to know that things are not always like they seem. There could be another reason. He should have gone back to question Charlie and maybe even leaned on him a little for not telling him. Maybe that would have stirred something up?

He gave Barb some instructions, asked her to see that the watch got over to Sheriff Conway and to have him call for disposition. He left for court with something still eating at him. *This episode is getting a little more interesting.* He sat in the hall at the court house and dug further into his notes about his meeting with Orin. As he read he remembered his feelings at the time that Orin was either lying or leaving something out. Orin had volunteered that Betty had gone home with Charlie and his family. Said she wasn't feeling good and Charlie volunteered to take her home. *What was Orin hiding?* Then he suddenly remembered the most important part of what had been bothering him. It was his final half legible scribble of the name Betty that triggered it. He couldn't get his leg to turn far enough around to kick his own rear end. He had the feeling he should have suspected foul play as a little more likely prospect. If this turned out to be anything he would feel bad for a long time. He already felt bad. He had depended on Orin Taylor to have his wife call him, and she never did. He had the feeling that was a mistake.

Buck's cell phone vibrated in his pocket, he always turned the ringer off when in a public building. "What's up with this watch Buck?" Sheriff Conway asked as soon as Buck keyed his cell phone on. Bill Conway was always a direct kind of guy.

"Hello, Bill. You remember the disappearance of that Thompson kid about five years ago? You were on the force then if I recall."

"Yeah, I remember. Kid drowned up on the Withla-coochee."

"Well we assumed he drowned. We never found the body to confirm it and I got to tell you that this watch brings up some interesting questions. I'd like you to send it to the lab and treat it as if it were a murder investigation. I doubt there would be any good prints on it except the recent ones, and every one in this county has handled it since it was found a few days ago."

"What are we looking for?"

"I don't know. For one thing, verify that it belongs to the missing boy. The serial number is on those insurance papers I put with it." Buck paused and added, "Look, Bill, I'll be honest with you, I may have dropped the ball on this one and I'd like to follow up with a hard investigation. Have them boys in forensic go over that watch with a fine tooth comb. It stopped on the date the boy disappeared and showed up in a spring a mile away from where his boat was found sunk."

"OK, Buck, but it won't be the boy's at forensic. There's a girl running that operation now, and from what I hear, she's a crackerjack. Her name's Elizabeth Morel."

That got a chuckle out of Buck. "Thanks, Bill, I got a couple of leads to follow up on and I'll keep you posted in case it gets over my head. I don't want to drop another ball."

"Fine, Buck, but if this turns into a murder investigation we'll have to get some detectives on it. Click."

Buck chuckled at Bill's directness. He never said goodbye, he just hung up when he was through. Buck wondered how long Bill would give him a free reign if this thing continued in the direction he suspected it was going? He had the ball now and wanted to carry it as far as he could. "Just don't drop it again." He said out loud.

Chapter Eleven

If the truth were known

Buck's cruiser left the paved road and vibrated along the washboard roads of Arrowhead subdivision towards Charlie's house. He knew Charlie was home because he had Barb call and tell Charlie to expect him. He wanted these questions to be answered face to face. He wanted to watch Charlie's eyes. He wanted not just the truth but the whole truth. He knew Charlie, and Buck's sense of judgment when it came to character was seldom wrong, but Charlie had failed to tell him something five years ago that could have been important. He had learned long ago that withholding information sometimes had the same effect as lying, if it was done deliberately. He was pretty sure that Charlie had not deliberately tried to mislead him but he wanted to know for sure. And he also wanted to know before he went to question Betty. He wondered if Orin had even told her to call him—probably not.

It had been an unusually dry winter and early spring and as he slowed for the turn into Charlie's drive the cloud of dust that had followed him down the road, caught and passed him filling his open windows. "Crap!" Buck exclaimed as he choked on the dust. He cursed himself for not closing his windows and using the air. He loved the outdoors and hated air-conditioning. It was only at times like this that he appreciated being closed in.

As he came to a stop Charlie came towards the cruiser with a grin on his face saying, "Stirred up a little dust, I see."

"Yeah, I forget to close my windows on these back roads till it's too late." Buck admitted with a sheepish smile on his face. "There ain't too many of these unpaved roads left in this county, at least ones that I travel much."

"What can I do for you, Buck? I haven't seen you in a spell."

Buck got out of the car and took a few minutes to beat the dust out of his hat before answering. He wanted to regain some of his dignity and impart a more serious air to this conversation before continuing. The silence did just that. He could see the seriousness creep over Charlie's face. Buck's instinct told him just when to begin. "Charlie," another pause, "you remember when that Thompson boy came up missin' some years back?"

"Yeah." said Charlie with a somber look on his face.

"Well I talked to you a day or so after and you told me that Orin Taylor and his wife Betty were there at the spring that evening."

"Yeah, that's right."

"You said that Orin left just before it got dark."

"Yep, right again." Charlie said with an uneasy shuffle to his feet, as if afraid of and knowing what was coming.

"What you didn't tell me was that Betty went home with *you* . . . not Orin." Buck said with a stern look on his face.

"I knew I shoulda told you Buck and I don't know why I didn't. It bothered me some right after that, but I really didn't see what that had to do with anything, and I would have told you if you had asked. I just felt sorry for Betty and didn't want to stir up any more trouble for her than she already had."

Buck had been watching Charlie's face and could see a shade of honest regret there. But it was also plain that there was more here than he had heard yet. "Well, Charlie," another pause for affect, "I am sorely disappointed that you didn't let me do the thinkin' about what was important and what wasn't important." He paused again just long enough, then said, "Charlie, I want you to tell me everything you know about that day at the spring and I don't want you to leave anything out cause you don't think it's important."

Charlie began with his wife's suggestion that they go to the spring for a late afternoon picnic. They drove there in the car as they usually did in cool weather instead of taking their powerboat. He continued and told him that Orin and his wife Betty were already there when they arrived. He mentioned that Orin was hitting the beer pretty heavy and getting belligerent as he usually did, that they ate and enjoyed the park like area while trying to ignore Orin.

"He even tried to pick a fight with me, but I mostly ignored him. I didn't want the wife and kids to see that kind of thing."

He told Buck about Betty and Orin having some kind of argument. "They started to get in the airboat and I saw him slap her in the face. I heard him say, 'Get your God-damn ass in the boat,' and saw him grab her by the arm. She jerked her arm free and backed out of his reach while the picnic basket she was carrying fell and spilled everything on the ground. I was movin' towards them to see if I could help her. Orin staggered towards her and tripped on the picnic basket. I woulda laughed like hell if he fell in the spring. He almost did. Betty let the basket lay there and ran over, askin' me to take her home."

"The wife and kids were already in the car." I said, "Sure Betty," then helped her in the car. Orin just stood there across the spring with his mouth hangin' open. I was hopin' he would come over then. I didn't care if the kids were watchin'. I cain't stand a man that treats a woman that way. I wouldn't of had any problem messin' him up some, the shape he was in."

"She was crying hard but seemed more determined and angry than afraid. She opened up on the way home and told us about her life with Orin. It must have been hell for her, living with that creep," said Charlie. "He beat her up several times. Not bad but bad enough that she was afraid of him. He would have these temper tantrums one day, then tell her how sorry he was the next. He would swear to her that he would never hit her again and the next few days or weeks he would seem like a changed man. Then just about the time she started to believe he had changed he would start the cycle again." Charlie told Buck why Betty said she didn't want to ride down the river with Orin, about him going too fast just to scare her sometimes, especially when he was drinking, and how she knew he would keep after her, until it led to violence, as it always did.

Buck kept quite while Charlie went on, letting him make up for not telling him the complete story before, by over-telling it this time. He was secretly anxious to leave, as he thought he had already heard everything important, then Charlie dropped another bomb.

Charlie continued, "She said she had had it. She was leaving him that night. She wanted to get there before he did, pack her clothes and get out before he came home. I asked her if she wanted me to hang around so he couldn't beat her up again. She said she would be OK. It wouldn't take her five minutes to pack. All she wanted was her clothes, some money she had tucked away, and her car, and she was out of there. She said she would hear his airboat coming from several miles away and would just leave if she heard him. I hung around anyway and he never came. I was surprised to think that you could spend several years in a house and relationship and walk out clean with a couple of suitcases and a car. I asked her about the house and she said he could have it. He owed more on it than it was worth."

"That's the last time I saw Betty. I know she left him that night, and I don't think she ever came back. I'm pretty sure she left town. I seen Gary over at the Seven Eleven later that week and he said she had quit and moved somewhere—he wouldn't say where, cause she asked him not to. And the last time I saw Orin he was blastin' away from Blue Spring."

"Excuse me, Charlie, did you say *blastin' away*?"

"Yeah, he took off with spray and leaves flying. We heard him loud and clear, even with the windows rolled up. He was pissed off for sure."

"I believe you said that was just before dark?"

"Yeah. It wasn't quite dark yet. I had to turn my lights on about the time I hit the main road."

Buck let that sink in for a while and realized that Charlie had finally finished completely. "Well, Charlie, I wish you had told me all this at the time. You're probably right; it may not mean much, but I still like to think I know most of what there is to know. I hate to get blindsided."

"Buck, I heard about that watch being found in the spring last week, and for some reason, me not telling you about Betty popped into my mind. What's all this mean? Are you re-openin' the investigation?"

"Look, Charlie, just because a watch was found in the spring don't mean we are openin' any kind of investigation. We have never had any reason to suspect that there was foul play involved with Jimmy's disappearance. You know this river as well as I do. Jimmy is not the first to come up missin' never to be heard from again. I'm just trying to fill in some blanks and I need the full story to do it." Buck paused, then turned to leave, "Thanks for your time, Charlie, and if you think of anything else, you know how to reach me. By the way, I would appreciate it if you would keep our little conversation under your hat."

Buck slid under the wheel, started the engine and drove out of Charlie's circular drive down the dusty road. His mind was whirling with what Charlie had just told him. He didn't realize until the stop sign at the paved road that his window was still down.

Chapter Twelve

Try, try again

He was on the radio as soon as he left Charlie's. Barb was to look in public records to find out if Betty was still married to Orin, and where she was if not. He was on his way to visit Orin but had no idea whether he was home or not. If he worked during the day he was likely to be getting home about this time. A phone call had produced no answer but he could be outside and didn't hear it.

Orin lived at the end of another one of those God-damned dirt roads and after the second load of dust today he had finally closed the windows and turned on the air. It was an unusually hot spring day. The air felt good but he knew he would suffer all the more when he got out of the car and stood in the heat. Getting in and out of air-conditioning always made it seem hotter than it really was. The Florida sun heated the asphalt roads hot enough, in the summer, to literally bake any stupid turtle that took too long to cross the road, and on those days he welcomed the relief his air-conditioning provided.

Orin's house came into view through a slot in the pines. There was a car in the drive. Buck waited for the dust to settle, got out and rang the door bell. *No answer.* He banged on the door with the heel of his hand and got no response. He walked around the house peeking in a window or two but saw no movement. *What a pig sty.* From the back of the house he could see the river with Orin's dock and boat house where he kept his airboat. What was the name of that boat? One of those suggestive names. Oh yeah, *Wet Dream.* The airboat was gone.

Buck decided to sit and wait on the dock in the cool shade the overhanging cypress trees provided. The river had a dark beauty that could lull you to sleep just looking at it. Buck's chin was on his chest and he was drooling when something woke him. He had no idea how long he had been asleep or what woke him until he finally noticed the distant buzz of an air boat getting louder. It turned from a buzz to a soul shaking roar and then into a deep rumble as he watched Orin approach his dock at idle speed.

Orin stiffened as he recognized Sheriff Stone, and mumbled to himself; "What the hell is he doing here?" It was too late to pretend he didn't see him, throttle up and leave him sittin' at the dock. He drifted in, tied off the boat and shut down the motor. "Evenin' sheriff, what brings you way out here?" Orin said with a strange look on his face, trying to be cool but not quite making it.

"Good evenin', Mr. Taylor. I was just in the neighborhood and thought of something I'd asked you to do for me." Buck was watching close and thought Orin was squirming. He waited a few moments while he watched Orin tie up the boat. He noticed the name on the transom, and thought to himself, Orin still had the same boat he had five years ago. When he got no response he continued. "I asked you to have your wife call me and you said you would." Orin was visibly squirming now.

"I haven't seen her since then," Orin replied, thinking hard.

"Why haven't you seen her?" Buck asked, knowing that they had gotten a divorce shortly after he had questioned Orin five years ago. Barb had called him back and given him the scoop. The divorce was initiated in the state of Washington where Betty was from and it was quite possible that he had not seen her.

"I just haven't seen her. She left me and went home to momma, or some other guy, or whatever. I don't rightly give a damn. And if you don't mind I have things to do and I'd like to get to them." he said with a touch of irritation showing along with his false courage.

"Well Mr. Taylor, I do mind. You see, I hate to be lied to and *you* are battin' about 500 percent in the lie department." He let that set in for a second and saw the show of bluster fade from Orin's countenance.

"What d'you mean? I never lied to you."

Buck smiled and said, "Then tell me again why your wife didn't ride home with you from Blue Spring the night that boy disappeared." Orin was sweating.

"I don't know. She wasn't feelin' good, that's all."

"It didn't have anything to do with your drinkin', and get-ting' rowdy?"

"Why don't you ask her?" Orin spat out, his face darkening.

"Tell me again how she left that morning before you got up, when she had actually been gone for two days," Buck said, ignoring Orin's question.

"Well, I was upset and it wasn't none of your business anyway." Orin said with the bluster returning.

"Oh yes Mr. Taylor, it was my business, especially since you were drunk at the spring, in a violent mood, and maybe the last person to see that boy alive, it was my business. I still would like to talk to your wife and hear her side of the story and I aim to do just that." He started to ask Orin for her address and phone number but knew Orin probably didn't have it and that he could get it without him.

"You said you went real slow on your way home that night?"

"That's right, I did." Indignation thickening his response.

"Well just when did you slow down?"

"What do ya mean?"

"You blasted away from Blue Spring at full throttle, so when did you slow down?"

"Who told you that?"

"Just answer my question."

"Well I slowed down right away, cause it was dark out and I had to use my light to see the river."

"It was my understanding that you left before dark."

"Well, you would just be wrong."

Buck turned to leave and then had a hunch. He turned back to Orin and said, "I noticed you came in from downriver and I've been talking to some of the regulars at Blue Spring. They haven't seen you there in a long, long time. Some say it's been about five years. Why is that Orin?"

The color drained from Orin's face and Buck knew he had just hit pay dirt. He never got an answer and didn't need one. He walked straight to his cruiser and drove away, his face flushed with anger.

Chapter Thirteen

Should'a, could'a, would'a

Buck still didn't have a clue as to what had happened that night. He was still trying to get his leg in position to kick himself for not being more aggressive from the beginning. *I know that damn Orin's involved up to his ass. I should have found and questioned Betty then. I should have been tougher acting with Charlie and I might've gotten the whole story from him then.* But he knew all that was water over the dam and that he couldn't rest until he knew everything about that night. He wrestled with how to proceed. He couldn't stir up anymore bad memories or false hopes for the Thompsons, yet he may need some piece of information they could contribute, no matter how trivial it may seem to them. Something they had perhaps told him but had no significance to him at the time. How can he get all the old facts back in his memory. His notes were only good when fresh in his mind but he would start by pouring over them again. He sometimes amazed himself remembering facts in cases, and then would leave his windows down on a dusty road. Who can I talk to without stirring up a hornets nest? Mike Tracy's maybe the best bet? Mike is good friends with the Thompsons and knew the boy real well. He had been there from the beginning and could probably tell me everything they could. But I'll have to do it in such a way as to not get Mike stirred up. He knew Mike could be volatile and didn't want to have Mike on the warpath. I'll have to question Mike without him knowin' it. It'll have to be a theoretical discussion.

Chapter Fourteen

If you only knew

Buck Stone sat at the bar stool, out of his uniform and Mike didn't recognize him until Buck said, "Hey, Mike, join me for a beer." Buck knew that Mike kept his boat here at Stumpys and he made a special effort to be here in plain clothes.

"I sure will, Buck. I'm like you, I can't drink while I'm working, but I just quit for the day and I am thirsty."

Buck had driven his own car so Mike wouldn't see it in the parking lot and think it was official business. Like Mike said, he had always made it a practice, a hard rule even, not to drink in uniform, but he knew Mike would feel more at ease over a beer. He knew what time Mike generally quit for the night and sat with a half gone glass of Amberbock when Mike came in.

Mike motioned to the bartender who was already on his way with a cold Amberbock, the dark beer that Mike favored. "I see you drink my brand too. What brings you here . . . in plain clothes even? I thought you slept in that uniform?"

Buck grinned and said, "What's the matter? You afraid I'll cut into your territory now that I'm single?"

"Hell no, Buck, there are plenty of women to go around and besides, you're way too old to give me any competition," Mike said with a grin.

"I wouldn't know what to do with a woman if I had one on my lap." Buck's wife had passed away some time ago, and conversation about Women didn't come easy to him, he guessed it wasn't quite long enough yet; it may never be. "I just had a night off and thought I would see what all the commotion was over at this place. I hear they serve mighty good catfish here and the beer is cold." Buck hesitated just long enough to make it sound spontaneous and said, "How about joining me for dinner? I hate to eat alone."

Buck had always respected Mike, and felt sure that the feeling was mutual. Mike was a straight shooter and there weren't too many of them around. He often thought Mike would be good company if you got to know him. I guess it boils down to respect, thought Buck. You could be friendly to those you didn't respect but you could never be true friends without respect. He thought that he and Mike could maybe be friends someday.

Mike finished his swallow of beer. He smiled at Buck and said, "Why sure Buck, I'll join you. I have some left over chili at home I intended to heat up, but it'll be even better tomorrow night."

They moved to a table, had another beer and ordered. Mike was the first to breach the subject of Jimmy, as Buck knew he would. "What'd you find out about The watch?"

"It's still in the lab, but I don't expect any surprises. I'm just as sure as you are it was Jimmy's watch and it did stop working on the night he disappeared just about sundown. The big mystery is how it got in the spring. I haven't a clue."

Mike was shaking his head. "I don't know either, but I'll tell you this; Jimmy didn't lose it there. He thought too much of that damn watch. Charlie Curtis and that fellow from down river . . . what's his name? Uh . . . Orin, I believe . . . yeah that's it. Orin Taylor. They both left the spring just before dark and neither of them saw Jimmy. Charlie said Jimmy wasn't at the spring all afternoon and that fellow Orin must have come down river right at dark. Did he see anything or was he driving that air boat of his so fast he couldn't see anything?"

"He said he didn't see anyone," Buck said, leaving out Orin's vague reference to someone coming downriver. "He said he went slow all the way home and that checked out with the Thompsons. They were fishing on their dock until they really got worried about Jimmy and they only heard one air boat, goin' slow down river, feelin' his way with his light. It had to have been Orin." Buck didn't offer to tell Mike about Orin being drunk or his own suspicion about Orin hiding something.

"Yeah," said Mike, "They went upstream looking for Jimmy right after that airboat went down river. It was black dark that night and they couldn't see the airboat, nothing but his lights,

49

but it had to be Orin. They were out there all evening and it was the only one they heard."

Something clicked in Buck's mind as Mike made that statement and he hoped it didn't show in his expression. If it was dark and they heard Orin going downstream just before they went upstream and neither of them saw Jimmy, where was he? It didn't make any sense. Something in the timing was wrong, dead wrong.

"What's wrong Buck?" Mike asked. "Did you just think of something else? "

"Naw, I was just thinking about the Thompsons," he lied. "I hope this watch thing don't bring all this up again for them." Mike looked long and hard at Buck and Buck knew he had been had.

The waitress brought their food and this created a natural lull in the conversation, but food or not, Buck was sure there would have been one. After a bite or two, Buck remarked that the catfish was the best he had tasted; it was prepared perfectly.

"Buck," Mike finally said, "you know something you're not telling me. I can only assume it's because you don't want me to pass it on and get the Thompsons all fired up again. . . . I got news for you good buddy, the Thompsons have relived that night, every night for five years. The only thing that will make this worse for them is for the 'not knowing' to continue. Every day that they sit and wonder what happened, puts one more nail in their coffin. I will not stop trying to find out what happened to Jimmy and if there is foul play involved, I will not stop until the son of a bitch responsible pays. So don't hold out on me," and the icy stare from those dark penetrating eyes continued.

Buck couldn't say anything more to Mike about his suspicions, but he knew Mike would soon put two and two together if he hadn't already. Buck didn't want Mike Tracy meddling in his business. "Mike, I don't know anything more than you. Sure, I got some ideas but I'm not in the idea business. I'm in the facts business. And I have no facts right now that lead to foul play." He wasn't going to tell him about Orin being drunk that night and his wife leaving him. He wasn't going to tell him that Orin left the spring like a bat out of hell, before it got dark. He wasn't going to tell him that Orin hadn't been back to the spring since that fateful night. All this was circumstantial and at best just implied that Orin could have been involved. Nor would he tell him that a preliminary study suggested that the water found inside the watch was river water not spring water—Hell, that wasn't a sure thing anyway. He himself wondered how river water entering through a tiny crack in the crystal could stay there five years while the watch was sunk in the clear water of the spring. But the lab technician said that the water was trapped there with no circulation—*what the hell do I know?* This offered the first probability that foul play was involved, and even that could have another possibility. *No,* he thought, *Mike may find these things out and come to the conclusion that there was foul play and maybe even who the prime candidate is, but he won't get it from me.*

They finished dinner in a cool fashion, shook hands and went their separate ways. Mike with a little steam coming from under his collar and Buck a little sad that he couldn't tell Mike everything.

Chapter Fifteen

What's going on?

The cool clear water ran in rivulets off his Florida Sun bronzed body as he agilely lifted himself onto their dock. Jenny watched with admiration and reflected on how close the three of them were. How much like a son Mike had become to her and Jim, especially since Jimmy's tragic disappearance. *Disappearance?* She knew in her heart that Jimmy was dead but sometimes her mind wouldn't let her acknowledge it. A lone marker down by the river and a memorial service with just the three of them was all she had to signify Jimmy's passing. She thought about Mike and how attached he had become to them.

Mike is a true loner. He is not a recluse, he likes being around people, certain people that is. Mike is usually ready to hit a bar or two and shoot a game of pool with a friend or join her and Jim for a night out at Stumpys, but he could happily tend his plants and piddle around the yard doing small household chores for days at a time by himself. He never spoke about family and for that matter made it plain he didn't want too. Something had separated them long ago and he is adept at working the subject away from that type of discussion. If you're someone he respects he will charm you away with some remotely related story of his youth which never includes his family. If you're one of his less favorite acquaintances, you're apt to get a short reply to any question in that area. She and Jim never questioned him, they saw from the beginning of their friendship that he was reluctant to discuss it. She figured he would tell them whatever there was to tell in his own sweet time. Later, as they got to know and respect each other, the stories would flow over their evening beer, but not about his early family life.

Mike was in his forties and had led a very active and varied life. He had worked the Texas oil fields in his youth, crewed on a small charter boat out of Clearwater, was part of a treasure hunt off Key West as a diver. He wore a gold chain with an authentic gold doubloon around his neck and she had never seen him without it. Mike sometime mentioned a girl named Annie who was part of that dive team and Jenny got the impression that if Mike ever had intentions of settling down with one girl it would have been Annie. He always described her with a tone of admiration in his voice. Told how she could dive with the best of them and was always ready for any adventure he could come up with, and from the number of stories Mike could tell, there were plenty of those.

Those years at Key West must have been good days for Mike. He had tended bar for several years after Key West and she thought that this was the least favorite part of his life. He spoke of it the least. His love for the river and all the wildlife made his decision to become a river guide the turning point in his life; he is happy now.

Jenny had learned from Mike, when he was in one of his more reflective moods, that he had considerable Indian blood in his family history. His great grandmother was a full blooded Cherokee. He seemed proud of that. There were indications of Indian heritage in his appearance. His dark eyes and easily tanned skin were subtle hints, and his shoulder length black hair which he usually kept in a pony tail, could reinforce the connection. He had a light beard and very little body hair. He was not often thought of as Indian by those whom he met, for his features were basically Caucasian. But the underlying image was there, and those who knew him well could see the traits in his character; the self reliance, the closeness to nature, the respect for the natural world and above all his loyalty to those close to him. The instinct to protect and help the center of his world (tribe) was plain to those near him.

Mike's stories of his somewhat volatile life kept her and Jim entertained and helped them understand the appeal of his life on the Withlacoochee. He had "been there, done that" and he didn't have to prove anything to anyone. His rowdy days on the oil fields had given him the confidence of knowing how to handle himself in a fight, and more importantly, how to get the fight over quickly with a minimum of damage on both sides. The hard physical life of his youth had hardened his body. His broad shoulders and lanky frame were well covered with rippling muscle, but his strength of character was somehow more intimidating than his physical stature. The deep, intense gleam of his dark eyes could warn another man that taking this disagreement any further would be a mistake.

There were instances Jenny knew of where this aura of invincibility had cowed a rowdy customer or made a boater who had violated Mike's rules of the river calmly listen to reason. The most powerful blows are sometimes those which are never struck. She knew Mike never sought violence, but that he knew how to deal with it when it came.

Crewing the charters with Captain Marley in Clearwater had started Mike's interest in conservation and taught him that even the vast ocean could be depleted of its treasures. Mike kept her and Jim spell bound with the retold tales of Captain Marley. Old Cap'n Marley had preached to Mike about the plentiful catches when as a young man he fished the skinny waters off Florida's west coast for trout, pompano, and redfish, for the most part feeding his family of five with a harvest from the sea. He related the old man's disgust at the diminishing population of those species as the brutal increase of netting and shrimping took its toll on the natural habitat and eventually destroyed the same industry it created like a snake eating its own tail. Captain Marley had always been a game fisherman and when he found out his talents for finding fish could extract big dollars from the city boys, he found himself with plenty of money and time for his family. He was one of the first guides to insist on a catch and release policy. He would only allow the chump—which he called them behind their backs—to keep one trophy fish or what went on the table. Even in the early 1900's he said he could detect the decline in certain species.

Mike told them about the old man watching the sea turtles' stoic march out of the surf in the moonlight, digging into the cool sand and laying her clutch of eggs, crawling feebly back to the protection of the sea before the Florida sun baked her in her own shell. He related the old man's sorrow at how high rise condominiums and man's invasion of the beaches took that and other natural wonders away from his children and grandchildren.

54

Cap'n Marley, as a charter boat captain, had lamented the steady decline of game fish; permit, snook, bonefish and the silver king tarpon. He had instilled in Mike a respect for all species and how they all fit together in one huge plan where even the smallest plays an important part.

The treasure hunting days at Key West had given Mike his fair share of adventure and excitement. He had learned how to deal with those who were dedicated to making you fail so that they might profit, whose respect for your well being or even your life was non-existent. He had also had the opportunity to work with those who would give their own life for you. Treasure has a way of bringing out the best and the worst in people. He said he felt lucky to have associated with some of the best. Kurt Daggot was one of those. Mike described Kurt as the best diver he had ever seen. Kurt could free dive to 50 feet and hang out there a minute or two. He didn't know the meaning of panic and zero visibility was just a slight handicap. Mike said he hadn't seen Kurt in years but knew that their bond extended beyond years and that if he ever needed him, he knew Kurt would be there for him, as he would for him.

Mike sauntered over towards Jenny still toweling off. "River's still cool." he remarked. "It's just about the temperature of the spring."

It's still too cool for me." said Jenny. "But it's getting there."

"Where's Jim today?" Mike asked.

"He's down to the Sheriff's office picking up the watch. I don't know what we'll do with it. Put it in a box I suppose?"

Mike said that Jim had not mentioned it to him. He said he would have been glad to drive down to Inverness with him. He always had something he needed at the hardware store or grocery. "How come you didn't go with him? I seldom see one of you without the other."

"He said he wanted to go alone. He didn't say why, but I figured the sheriff asked him to come alone." She said with a quizzical look on her face. "He probably thought I would break down and start bawling when they handed us the watch."

"What time's he getting back?" Mike asked.

"He should be back anytime now," she replied.

"Well, I'll catch you later. I have to get a boat out tonight for some maintenance work. Tell Jim to call me when he gets back I might need some help."

"OK, Mike," Jenny said.

Chapter Sixteen

The need to know

After Mike left Jenny he went inside and sat down. Mike thought to himself, *what's that damn sheriff up to now?* He thought about Jim being called to the sheriff's office alone and knew something was up. He had to figure out what. He knew it had something to do with the watch. Whatever it was, Buck was going to soft peddle it to Jim and hope he didn't get any static. *He's going to swear Jim to secrecy, but I'll get it out of Jim.* He had not wanted Jenny there. *Why?* Jenny was perceived to be perhaps a little fragile by Buck and Buck knew Jim could soften any news that might otherwise get her hopes up falsely. *He had not wanted me there. Why? He perceives me as a hot head and didn't want me to go off half cocked.* "Well I won't go off half cocked; I'll just find out what he won't tell me and go off fully cocked, with the safety off," he said out loud.

He showered and fixed a bite to eat, watched the news and waited for Jim's call. He didn't really need Jim's help tonight but he wanted to quiz him about his visit to the sheriff's office. The phone rang and it was Jim. "Hi, Jim, can you come over and give me a hand? I want to move a boat and I could use some help."

"Sure, Mike, right now?"

"Yeah, now's fine if it suits you."

"I'll be right over. Give me five minutes."

Five minutes later Jim was knocking on the door. Mike let him in and explained that he needed someone to ride with him to Stumpy's, and then drive to meet him at the boat ramp. Mike was being cautious and wanted Jim to volunteer the information he sought. He figured Jim would open up to him once they got to talking. "Jenny said you went down to see Buck."

"Yeah, he wanted me to tell me he was keepin' the watch for awhile."

Mike thought Jim wasn't telling him everything. "Anything new?"

Jim was silent for a long time as if contemplating what if anything he would say. Then with a broken voice he said, "Buck asked me to keep this from you, and I said I couldn't do that. He said you would read too much into it and that he didn't want you to stir up trouble, and maybe you will read too much into it, but what the hell. Isn't that better than not reading enough into it . . . and I got to tell you . . . I know he feels like he read too little into it five years ago. I can smell the guilt on his conscience." Jim took a deep breath and continued. "We all knew the watch stopped working about the time Jimmy was supposed to come home. They examined the watch very carefully and found two very interesting things. That watch suffered a severe blow which stopped it and cracked the crystal allowing the watch to fill with water." He paused as if to catch his breath then said, "Mike," and his voice broke again, "it was filled with river water."

"How could they tell?"

"It was mainly the tannin. The river water is a different composition than the spring water. It seems that this is standard procedure for them. Like in drownings, to make sure the victim drowned where they were supposed to have drowned. Buck said you could even tell by eye if you looked close at a sample of each."

"But how did the river water stay there that long?

"I asked the same question," said Jim, "and Buck said the watch had to be full of water when it was thrown or dropped in the spring, there was no pressure differential and since the crack was minute there was no circulation."

Mike sat speechless while he let the full impact of this knowledge sink in. His mind was racing and searching for a logical explanation for the watch being in the spring and could think of none. Try as he might he could not think of a single possibility of Jimmy damaging the watch and then tossing it in the spring. Some kid who didn't respect the things that were given him, who had too much disposable stuff, so much that he lost respect for those things, may have damaged the watch by accident and just tossed it, but not Jimmy. The watch just turning up in the spring was enough for Mike to suspect foul play, and he thought Jim felt the same way before his visit to the sheriff's office. Now he knew that was the case and he knew Jim knew as well.

Jimmy hadn't had much stuff after his parents died. When the dust of probate had settled with all the debts paid and auctions finished there wasn't much left over to help raise him. The proceeds from the sale of the house left Jimmy with a trust fund sufficient to get him through college if he brought in extra money to live on. Jim and Jenny had given him all the love that his parents could no longer give but they couldn't give him things. The everyday cost of just raising jimmy was a strain on their budget. Jimmy knew this and cherished anything and everything they did give him. When they gave him his first good casting rod and reel, Jimmy was street smart enough to know that it was more than they could afford on their fixed income. He was so proud of it he rode his bike all the way to Stumpys to show Mike. He cherished that rod and reel as he did all of his meager possessions. He would wipe off the rod with fresh water, clean and oil the reel after each day of fishing. He treated his lures much the same way. He would take extra pains to retrieve them when he would cast a bit too far and got hung in a tree for he knew he would have a hard time replacing them. He would even save the treble hooks on worn out or broken lures to replace the ones on his favorite lures when they got dull, broken or rusty. Mike admired his respect for the things he had. And Mike knew as did Jim and Jenny that that watch of his dads was his most cherished possession. He would never have thrown it away even if he had broken it.

Jim was reluctant to speak for he knew what was going though Mikes mind. It had been the same with him at the sheriff's office. Finally he said in a quiet voice, "I'm going to have a hard time keeping this from Jenny and I don't even know if I should. You know all those pictures she takes on the river? The ones of the cypress knees and the swamp. She has been doing that since Jimmy's disappearance. Mike, I think sometimes she is still looking for Jimmy. I know it's crazy and yet I also know she's not crazy. She needs to know what happened worse than anybody. It's an unfinished thing. I see her sometimes going over a particular photo that she took with a magnifying glass. What do you suppose she is looking for?" Jim paused then continued. He expected no answer.

"You know what she is looking for? . . . Nothing. . . . She doesn't expect to find anything, she just has to look."

Mike knew what Jim was talking about. He could see the melancholy set in ever so often and she would get her camera and kayak and paddle off up or down the river. She rarely showed him her photos although most of them were very good. And when she did show them they were very repetitious. It was uncanny that with all the wildlife and beauty around the river that she seemed to concentrate on the river banks. Her earlier photos were stunning and captured the mood of the river. Both he and Jim had encouraged her to show them formally but she said it wasn't something she wanted to do. She would smile that smile that says, "This conversation is over," then say, "Maybe someday."

"This is crazy," exclaimed Mike. "It doesn't make any sense. Who saw him last? Where was he then? The watch stopped at five fifty-eight where was Jimmy then? Was he fishing in the river, or did he tie up to that tree later? What happened at that tree? There were no marks of a collision on the boat, they found most of his stuff. Why did the boat sink? If Jimmy just fell out of the boat he would have climbed back in. He could have swamped the boat trying to climb back in but he could have swam to shore or climbed up on a limb of the tree. He would done any one of those things unless he banged his head and lost consciousness. Where was his life preserver? He had it with him. He must have had it on? The only two things that turned up missing were Jimmy and his life preserver," Mike paused.

"I don't know the answer to a single one of those questions," said Jim sadly. "I wish I did."

"You do what you think best about telling Jenny, but I will say this Jim; she's a strong gal and she will survive either way. Just let me know now so I don't put my foot in my mouth." and Mike looked him straight in the eye, waiting for the answer.

Jim rubbed his forehead while examining the weave of Mike's carpet then said in a pained voice, "I'm going to tell her everything Mike."

"Great," said Mike, "I knew you would, I just didn't want to interfere. She deserves to know. When she's had time to digest the news I would like to discuss it with the both of you. How long do you think?"

"Oh, I guess tomorrow," he said in a heavy voice. "I guess we better get your boat moved now?" said Jim.

"Aw, that's OK," said Mike, "I'll get someone at Stumpys to drive my truck over to the ramp. It only takes a few minutes. I guess you need to go talk to Jenny now anyway?"

"I figured you just wanted to talk," said Jim, "You usually don't need me to move your boat, but I'll be glad to help if you do."

"Thanks Jim, but I can get it OK without you. Go talk to Jenny, you need each other."

Mike sat in silence, thinking about what Jim had said. That had to be the secret Buck had kept from him the other night. He could understand why Buck kept it from him if he hadn't told Jim and Jenny. *What else was he keeping from him, or from them for that matter?*

Chapter Seventeen

Do you really want to know?

Jenny was holding dinner and waiting for Jim when he came in. "Wow, that didn't take long. I expected you to be at least another hour."

"Well, it turned out Mike didn't really need me. He just wanted to talk."

"It takes a good bit to get Mike in a talking mood," she quipped, "what's up with him?"

"Its about my visit with the sheriff today."

"I thought Mike would try to find out what was going on. It was pretty mysterious of Buck to invite you down there alone. He should have known it would stir Mike's curiosity, if he found out. It had me wondering too, but I knew you would tell me sooner or later. You men have to protect the womenfolk. I guess Mike couldn't wait for you to take your sweet time?" and she started setting the table for dinner.

"No, Mike couldn't wait so I told him, and I'll tell you right after we eat," he said in a light manner so as to ease the tension until after dinner. He thought that if he told her now, she wouldn't eat and he probably wouldn't either. As it turned out, they neither one ate very much anyway they just picked at their food and tried to make small talk, but they both were lost in their own thoughts. Jim was figuring out just how to tell her and Jenny was speculating and somehow dreading what Jim was about to tell her. Jim reckoned he had made a mistake by waiting.

Jim said, "Jenny let's sit out on the porch and have a glass of wine? We can get the dishes later."

"Fine," said Jenny, "I'll get the wine.   We have some great *Beaujolais* open.

Jim left the table and went to the porch where the soft light from the kitchen and the glow of a good glass of wine would ease his torment.

Jim told Jenny about the water in the watch, about the sharp blow stopping it and about the conversation he and Mike had. He told her that Mike wanted to get together and discuss it if she was up to it.

"He said we needed some answers and didn't think Buck Stone was going to give them to us, and I think he's right. Buck was looking mighty sheepish about something."

All through dinner Jenny had imagined what it could be the sheriff didn't want her to hear, and what she heard now was no worse than what she had imagined. Any thoughts of Jimmy still brought a lump to her throat.   She reckoned it always would.   Time had enabled her to control it, to where it didn't show, but it wasn't always like that.   Sometimes she would just break down and cry until the pain subsided.   She blamed herself for letting him roam the river by himself, and the pain from this hurt deep in her heart until she slowly came to realize that she couldn't have kept him from the river. He loved the river, loved fishing, loved being alone, all these things were part of Jimmy. Take away the river and it would kill the Jimmy she knew. It wasn't the river that took Jimmy from her. She was starting to realize it was *someone*.

She, like Jim and everyone else had thought of it as an accident, but it had haunted her like a recurring bad dream. It was like where you fall and fall but never hit the ground; you wake up, and when you go back to sleep you fall all over again. She was tired of falling. She was tired of paddling up the river with her camera and not being able to allow herself to click the shutter on anything but every little hunk of junk lodged in the cypress knees, or some hollowed out spot in the bank where some gator had dragged something. She knew when she took the photos that they were nothing, but to her it was doing something. She didn't take many pictures anymore.   She still paddled up the river and searched the banks, for what she didn't know. But the futility of her actions was not unknown to her. She sensed that Jim had it all figured out as well and that it bothered him. She hoped Mike was right, maybe they could find some answers.

Chapter Eighteen

I was afraid of that

Buck Stone wanted to fly to Everett, Washington and talk to Betty Manning, Orin's wife of five years ago. He could use a little vacation, but his current workload and budget wouldn't allow it. It would have to be a phone call. Barb had located her through records several days ago and he kept thinking he could find time to fly out there but it didn't happen. He sat at his desk in his favorite thinking position with his head in his hands and elbows on the scarred oak surface, his eyes closed in concentration. He was going over his notes which were directly in front of his closed eyes. He would open his eyes occasionally and leaf through for some bit of information pertinent to his present line of thought which was what could Betty add to what he knew, or could she fill in some blanks? She was there that night but not with Orin on his trip downriver. She could collaborate Charlie's story of why she chose to ride with him. And she could testify as to Orin's condition during that trip which Buck thought was angry and drunk. *Did she see Orin again that night? Did she know about Jimmy being missing? Could that have had anything to do with her leaving Orin for good?* He wanted to see her face when he asked these and other questions. He would know if her answers were truthful. He could maybe tell over the phone if she hesitated in her answers or tried to qualify her replies. Some liars were good, they usually had a lot of practice, but their tangled webs seemed always to catch them up. What he had heard about Betty didn't seem to put her in that category. He really didn't think she had anything to hide. According to Charlie she was determined to be out of there before Orin made it home. Well, if it felt wrong he could always go to see her.

The time difference put it about 6:00 PM in Washington as he dialed the number. It rang a few times and he was beginning to think she wasn't in when a breathless voice said, "Hello."

"Well hello, I thought you might not be home, it rang so long."

"Oh, I'm sorry, I was out in the back yard playing with my dog, Rusty. Who is this?"

Buck introduced himself as a Citrus County Deputy Sheriff and paused to see how she would react.

She was still out of breath but replied fairly quickly, "Is this call about Orin Taylor?" There was a certain hardness in this question which Buck detected.

"Yes, ma'am, it is. I would like to ask you a few questions if you don't mind?"

"Sheriff, I haven't seen Orin for over five years and if I never see him again it will be too soon." He could feel her hatred for this man across three thousand miles of phone wires.

"Yes, ma'am, but what I want to know took place over five years ago and I think you can help me."

She agreed to answer his questions, excused herself to let Rusty inside then told Buck he could continue. Buck questioned her first about her relationship with Orin and got what he thought was a straight story. A story of a frustrating life of being used and abused, of his drinking habits and temper when he drank. When asked why she put up with it so long she replied, "I wish I knew. I guess I'm just too gullible, thinking someone can change. He had his moments and at the time I thought I needed him. I believed his promises to change. He would break down and beg me to stay with him. He was very persuasive."

She went on to confirm all that Charlie had told him, and said she had not seen him since she left him at Blue Spring. When asked about Jimmy she said she had heard about a boy being missing about the time she left but didn't know how it came out, whether or not they ever found him.

"They never found him, ma'am. And I need to know something that I think you would know and I hope you will tell me. There's no use beatin' around the bush, I think Orin had something to do with the boy's disappearance. I am pretty sure he was the last one to see the boy alive and he's lyin' about that and other things about his trip down the river that night. Now what I

66

need to know is this . . . ," and he paused to catch a deep breath then continued. "If you suppose for a minute that Orin hurt that boy or maybe even killed him, by accident, would he have had the guts to face up to it or would he go to great lengths to cover it up?"

She was taken by surprise and it took her a minute to answer, but when she did, it was with great deliberation and as Sheriff Stone listened he knew he was talking to the right person. She spoke softly. "I want to tell you, sheriff, that I don't know anything that would indicate that Orin had anything to do with that boy's death. But I also want to tell you, yes to both your supposition and question. I don't hold anything against Orin for my troubles with him. It was entirely my fault. I could have left anytime and should have left the first time I saw Orin's dark side. He did have a dark side that came out mostly when he was drinking. And he was certainly drinking that night. I had learned to recognize the signs of trouble and avoid him when I saw it coming on. First Orin would get belligerent and sometimes when things were going all his way he would later mellow out. But let the least bit go wrong and he would fly off the handle. Orin grew violent and would lose control. He would throw things, hit me if I was around causing him trouble and if he was driving his car or that damn airboat he would drive too fast and reckless. So yes, he could have hurt that boy that night, he was in his violent stage. He struck me in the face, and twisted my arm so hard I dropped our picnic basket, that's why I left with Charlie. If he hadn't stumbled when I ran after Charlie he would have beat me hard right then. When he saw he couldn't catch me, he left the picnic basket mess and stumbled into his airboat. That was the last time I ever saw him. As Charlie drove off I heard him take off down river really fast, and I was so glad I wasn't with him."

"Excuse me Betty, but he said he drove the airboat home just above idle cause it was so dark that night. I just want to make sure that he wasn't goin' slow, like he claimed. It was dark; there was no moon that night."

"All I know is he pulled out of Blue Spring like a bat out of hell. I heard him in Charlie's car with the windows rolled up and the kids hollering at each other. There was still a little light when we left," she added, and I can assure you he wouldn't have slowed down unless something happened—to him or his boat.

This confirmed what Charlie had said the second time around. He cursed Charlie under his breath for not saying all this when he first questioned him—*damn him.*

"And I can tell you that if there was an accident and Orin did hurt that boy, he would take a coward's way out. He's a devious person and will do or say anything to protect this image he has of himself. I sometimes think he even lies to himself after doing something wrong or stupid, to the point where he believes his own lies. I don't know if Orin had anything to do with that boy's disappearance but if he did he will cover it up if he can."

"Yes, ma'am, I believe he has done a good job of that for five years." He thanked her for being a big help, wished her well and started to say goodbye when his memory kicked in again. He was certain before he talked to Betty that Orin had a great deal to do with Jimmy's disappearance. Now, after his conversation with her he was double sure that Orin had a great deal to do with Jimmy's death as well. This connection with an airboat caused him to remember something else that had turned up in the search for Jimmy's body. "Ma'am, I forgot something. Just two more questions if you don't mind."

"Surely," she replied.

"Did Orin wear earmuffs when he drove his airboat?"

"Oh yes, he had a bright yellow pair that he bought at a yard sale. I believe they were Navy surplus, used by a flight crew on an aircraft carrier around the jet engines or something."

"Thanks ma'am, you have been real helpful and I truly appreciate it."

And before he could hang up she asked, "What was the other question?"

"You've already answered it ma'am. I wanted to know what color they were. Thanks again and goodbye."

Buck hung up the phone and resumed his thinking position. It was starting to come together. He now knew that Orin was covering up for sure and that the timing was such that he had to be the last one to see Jimmy alive. It was a sure bet that he had something to do with his death. The hang-up was the missing body. *Why wasn't the body ever found?* He had asked himself this question a hundred times and he now thought he might have at least part of an answer. If there was an accident, would that bastard be callous enough and stupid enough to hide the body?

From what he had just heard, he thought so. The only way to know for sure is find the body. He could put pressure on Orin and maybe get a confession. Get him to tell him where it was and hope there was enough left to discover. He needed some leverage. He knew he didn't have enough to force a confession at this point. She had given him what could be an important link with the yellow earmuffs. They were probably Orin's. He was sure they were cataloged and properly photographed when the diver had found them but he also knew it was just another piece of worthless, circumstantial evidence. Orin could claim he dropped the earmuffs by accident on his way home that night. He wanted this asshole bad, but five years of cold trail was hard to follow.

Chapter Nineteen

Let's catch up

Jim, Jenny, and Mike were sitting at Jenny's round table. Jenny had opened beers for everyone and there had been some small talk. Then sensing that he would have to be the one to break the ice, Mike started the conversation towards Jimmy's disappearance. Jenny had a yellow legal pad and had a list of questions written down. They were pretty much the same ones that Mike had voiced to Jim two days ago, with some new ones added. They started taking the questions one by one just to see if one of them knew anything that another didn't. When they came up with a possible answer they would write it down.

The questions of course were centered around the events of that fateful night. Since Mike had not gotten involved until later that night, he didn't have much to contribute, just a different view of things.

The first and most important question was who had seen Jimmy last that day and the only answer they could come up with was that Orin Taylor may have seen him last. George Upton could have seen him last, from his kitchen window. George's house was way upstream from the spring, and from where Jimmy's boat was found, so what ever had happened, happened some time after George had seen him. Orin was in the right place at the right time to have seen him. Jenny and Jim could not pinpoint the time that they heard Orin on his way home, but they were sure it was after dark. They knew that Charlie was at the spring and hadn't seen Jimmy. He had said there were no kids there all afternoon and he didn't leave until just before dark. They also knew that Orin had left the spring about the same time. They had heard from Charlie, back when it happened that Orin was there with his wife, they didn't know her name. She would have been with Orin and could have seen Jimmy even if Orin didn't. They had to assume that the sheriff had questioned all these people and that none of them had seen Jimmy. *Buck wouldn't keep it from him if he had found that one of them had seen Jimmy, would he?* So they put the answer as Orin Taylor and his wife.

The second question was easy; How did the watch get into the spring? The only answer led them to the next most difficult question. They knew someone threw it there but who? Whoever threw it there didn't want it to be found. Whoever it was knew that no one swam there in the early spring and it would surely be covered with sand by summer. So this person had something to hide. They were definitely involved in whatever happened to Jimmy.

The answer to the second question was that someone threw it, and the answer to the third was, a suspect. A suspect for what? This was a question which had always been the basis of their search. What happened? If someone did a foul deed, what exactly was it? They knew full well the results of that deed. Jimmy was missing; did someone kidnap him, or murder him and hide the body? They all knew they would have to face that answer one day and it looked like this was the day.

Jenny said with tears in her eyes, "Why would anyone want to kidnap or murder Jimmy?"

Mike and Jim were looking at each other and thinking the same thing. "They wouldn't Honey. They just wouldn't." Jim said, as he continued to look at Mike.

"That's right Jenny. Jim's right, they wouldn't." Mike took a long pull at his beer which had just been setting there until now. "The only thing that makes sense is an accident, which is what we thought all along. Only now we have someone else involved who wants to cover it up. It's starting to make sense. I wonder if Buck is this far along?"

"That would explain the guilty look he was trying to hide," said Jim. "The watch is the give away. It's the only thing that leads to foul play and he didn't have that at the time. That's why he feels guilty. He knows now he should have dug deeper."

"Yeah, hind sight's 20/20," agreed Mike. "Hell, no one suspected foul play."

"And that leads right back to who?" Jim remarked.

"If that man and his wife came down the river before the accident they would have seen Jimmy fishing. If they came down after the accident and the boat was sunk, it looks like they would've seen something," Jenny remarked. "Especially if they were going slow. All of Jimmy's gear would have been floating around. Most of it had washed up under the cypress knees by the time we started looking."

"There's something missing here. The timing is not right." Mike paused, then asked, "you said it was after dark when you heard the airboat coming downriver? Was it well after dark or just after?"

"It was well after as I recall," Jenny said, looking at Jim for confirmation.

"Yeah," said Jim, "that's the way I remember it."

"How long after that did you leave to look for him?"

"Not long," Jim replied, "we had stopped fishing and were getting pretty worried. It couldn't have been more than five or ten minutes."

"It was not like Jimmy to be that late without a good reason," Jenny interjected.

"Did you hear any other boats after that?"

"No," Jim said, "we were listening hard for Jimmy's little motor and heard nothing."

"Then the accident had to have been over by then," Mike stated, "The watch had to have been part of the accident and it stopped at five fifty-eight. That's before it gets real dark, and it's not that far from here to the spring. Why didn't Orin or his wife see something? If it happened just minutes before they came down river, how could someone else have gotten past them upriver without them seeing them? It just doesn't add up."

"Yeah, and I'll bet Buck's closer to having an answer than we are." Jim added.

"Another thing," Mike said, "If this Orin fellow left the spring before dark and didn't pass here until well after dark, he must've been going damn slow."

Mike thought about all this as he finished his beer in silence. Jim and Jenny were each lost in their own thoughts. Mike was way ahead of them with his future plans. He was going to talk to Charlie. Charlie knew this Orin fellow and Mike wanted to know more about him.

Chapter Twenty

It's never too late

Charlie was cutting grass when Mike pulled in the drive. He noticed that Mike had the sense to keep his windows up on this dusty road. It was more than he could say for the sheriff who had been there a couple of days ago. Buck must've had a wheelbarrow load of dust inside that car, he thought.

Charlie knew Captain Mike but not very well. He stopped his lawnmower and approached Mike's truck while openly admiring it. "Nice truck you got there Mike. I've often thought I would like something like it."

"Thanks for the compliment, Charlie. I built her up myself from a pile of rusted parts."

"She sure sounds good."

"Yeah, she's a little better than stock and I keep her well tuned."

"What brings you over here, Mike?" Charlie asked.

Mike knew only one way and that was getting to the point. "What do you know about Orin Taylor?"

"Damn," Charlie said, "I need to write this down and make copies."

"What do you mean?" asked Mike with an innocent look on his face, but thinking he knew, (The sheriff had already been here).

"Well, I'll tell you what. Why don't we go inside out of this sun and I'll get the missus to fix us a glass of iced tea."

"Sounds like a start," Mike said with a grin.

They went inside to a neat, homey living room and Charlie called out to his wife, "Helen, You got any tea made? We got company."

"Sure, Hon, I'll bring some in. Who's here?"

"It's Mike Tracy." He turned and looked hard at Mike. "I guess I know what this is about. It's not hard to figure that Orin's mixed up in the disappearance of that Thompson boy with all the interest in him since that watch turned up. However, I got to tell you that Sheriff Stone asked me to keep it quiet. What I told him, that is."

"What did you tell him?"

"Well now, that wouldn't exactly be keeping it quiet would it?"

"Just ask yourself, what could it hurt? Did he ask you not to tell me specifically?"

"No."

"You have my word that whatever you tell me will not go any further. I swear I will not breathe a word to anyone else. No one will know that I talked to you."

"Well, there's not much to tell," he said as Helen arrived with the iced tea. "Helen, you remember Captain Mike Tracy from the Christmas party at the clubhouse a year or so back?"

"Yes, I remember that cute girl you brought and how you two stole the show on the dance floor," she added with a smile. "What ever happened to her? I thought you two would be married by now?"

"Oh, she's still around. I see her every now and then," he said in an unconcerned manner, not wanting to get into why they weren't married. She took the hint and excused herself as having chores to do, telling them to call for more tea.

Mike took a swallow of tea, remarked how good it was loud enough for Helen to hear. Then turned to Charlie and asked, "What kind of guy is this Orin?"

"Well, he drinks a lot, drives his airboat too fast, is an overbearing, loudmouth S.O.B., but other than that, he's a nice guy. He lives down on the river just south of Stumpknockers. He works in Ocala in construction, I don't know exactly what he does."

"Does he come up to Blue Spring often?"

"He used to, but come to think of it, I haven't seen him there in quite a spell. It's been years since I've seen him at the spring."

"I heard he was married?"

"He's single now. He was married, but she left him about five years ago. As a matter of fact, it was the night of the boy's disappearance that she left him for good. She left him on more than one occasion. I heard he would get violent when he got to drinkin' and somethin' didn't go just right. She sometimes didn't leave in time and he would take his anger out on her. I knew her from the Seven Eleven over in Homosassa; she worked there. Sometimes she would show up at work looking like she had been in an automobile wreck. Gary, the manager said it was her husband that did it."

"I understand Orin was at the spring the day that Jimmy disappeared and that his wife was with him? What was her name?"

"Her name was Betty. She was with him that day alright; at least she came with him." Charlie remarked.

"What do you mean, came with him?" Mike asked as the hair on the back of his neck began to tingle. *What the hell is going on?*

"I mean she didn't leave with him," he said. "She asked me to take her home and I did. Orin blasted out of there just before dark calling her a bitch. Orin had been drinking quite a bit and she didn't want to ride home with him. She said he scared her on the river at night, he drove it too fast and usually without a light, and when he did use the light it bounced off the trees and disoriented her. On the way home, she said she was going to leave him that night. She swore she would leave him for good this time, and I guess she did, for she wasn't at the Seven Eleven that next week. Gary said she quit without notice, even left without picking up her last check. He had to send it to her a couple of weeks later. When she gave him the new address, she asked him not to tell Orin. Gary said he was glad to oblige. He didn't like the son of a bitch either. He said to me, 'That bastard had the gall to come in and ask for *her* check.' Ain't that somethin?"

Mike had heard Charlie and registered all he had to say but the first words he had heard ('She didn't leave with him . . . Orin blasted out of there'), were overpowering everything else. If this guy blasted out of there as Charlie said he would have been way past Jim & Jenny's house when they said they heard him go by. "When did you tell Buck this?" he asked.

"Just a couple of days ago. He seemed to know it already."

"You mean you didn't tell him this five years ago?"

"No, I didn't think it was important then," he said defensively, "and I still don't see how it could be. You want some more tea?"

Mike stared at Charlie for longer than was comfortable for Charlie, then coolly said, "No thanks, I've got to go." And without explanation rose and walked towards the front door.

Charlie rose, opened the door and stood awkwardly as Mike walked out. "What's the matter Mike? Did I say something wrong?" asked Charlie.

"No Charlie, you didn't say anything wrong." Mike's penetrating eyes locked onto Charlie's. "You just said it too late." and he turned and walked away before Charlie, who stood there with his mouth open, could reply. The gravel flew and the dust cloud drifted towards Charlie as Mike's Chevy truck roared out of sight.

Chapter Twenty-one

What you don't know won't hurt you!

Mike was seething as he jumped into his pickup, slammed the door, and roared out of Charlie's drive in a cloud of dust. His mind was working hard to digest all that he had just heard. His thoughts were coming rapid fire. *That dumb ass.* He couldn't believe Charlie didn't tell Buck all that shit five years ago. *That means that Orin was alone on the river. He left in a huff. Blasted away before dark, and Charlie had said he had been drinking. If Orin left before dark why did it take so long for him to pass the Thompson's house? It wasn't that far downriver. Jesus Christ, the puzzle was clearing up. Why did Orin slow down before he passed the Thompson's?* He thought he knew now. *But how did the watch get off Jimmy's arm and into the spring?* He didn't know how it got off Jimmy's arm, but he was damn sure he knew *who* threw it into the spring and he was determined to find out *why*—Orin Taylor was about to meet Mike Tracy.

Chapter Twenty-two

Contact!

Mike was thirty feet under the surface in the hold of wreck with a tangle of wire and loose line tugging at his regulator and back pack. He was struggling to free himself and trying to suck more air out of his empty tanks when he first heard the ringing. "Where in the hell was a phone down here?" He woke up with the phone cord hooked in his arm and the phone on the floor. He had come home exhausted and plopped into his recliner to rest before fixing dinner. By 9:30, the long day and a couple of beers had pulled his eye lids shut.

He pulled the phone towards him and paused, hearing words out of the receiver saying "Hello, hello." His brain started functioning and he said, "Hello, Captain Mike's Lazy River Cruises, Captain Mike speaking."

"Are you the guy down at the Crossroads tonight, looking for information?" an unfamiliar voice questioned.

Mike thought to himself, this must be the Billy that Allan spoke of.

It was Mike's busy season but he had been doing a little socializing on the side trying to get a line on Orin Taylor. He had been talking to several people who might know him. Tonight he had gone bar hopping in Orin's neighborhood and hit pay-dirt. The Crossroads Bar & Grill was a favorite hangout for some of the airboat crowd and had a couple of pool tables. He knew the bartender Allan from way back when they had both worked the same bar in St. Petersburg. Mike had told him he had an interest in Orin Taylor and needed some names of Orin's friends.

Allan had said, "Orin doesn't have any friends. He comes in here and plays pool, but he usually comes in by himself and he usually drinks by himself. Sometimes he brings a girl, but rarely the same one more than two or three times. He sometimes hangs with a fellow named Bobby who owns a parts place right up the road, but they don't seem to be good friends. They talk a lot but it seems to be serious stuff they talk about. They sometimes argue and when they do, they talk reeeeal quiet and look around as if someone was listening."

"Sounds like a real sociable guy."

"What do you want from a guy like that, Mike?"

"I'm just trying to get a line on him. I got him pegged as a real asshole and he may have been involved in a bad scene a few years ago which I have an interest in. I need some way to get inside this guy."

"I do know someone who may be able to help you. He's done some side jobs for Orin and his wife works for Bobby, the guy that hangs with Orin sometimes. He's a talker and he always has a few things to say about Bobby when he gets a snoot full. I usually don't pay much attention. You know how it is in this business. Guys come in here spilling their guts and I've heard it a hundred times. It goes in one ear and out the other."

"Yeah I know. I used to get in a zone where I could actually carry on a conversation with a chump and my mind would be elsewhere. Most of my contributions to the conversation would be, 'yeah' or 'no kidding' or 'is that so?' but it made no difference to the chump, he just kept right on talking."

"This guy's name is Billy something or other, I don't know his last name. He works the afternoon shift at the van conversion place up on I-75. Usually comes in here by himself after work a couple of times a week. He acts as if he's a big shit and knows something on this Bobby and I think it has somethin to do with Orin. I don't give a shit what he knows, so I don't give him an opening to tell me. I just brush it off and change the subject to baseball or something else I've already recorded in my brain cells. You know what I mean?"

"Yeah, you want to stay in a zone."

"You got that right. This shit gets old after twenty years."

"Yeah, I know. That's why I quit and moved up here in Nowhereville. And I wouldn't go back."

Allan said he would talk to Billy whenever he saw him and would see if he could get him to talk to Mike. Mike said he would make it worth Billy's while if he had something useful and Allan had said he would have him get in touch if he could.

This must be Billy on the phone, mike thought, Allan didn't mention anyone else. He didn't expect action this soon. "Who is this?" Mike said rather curtly.

"I understand you are in the market for information," the caller said in a conspiratorial tone.

"Cut the bullshit asshole. If we are going to have any further conversation you're going to come on straight with me. I asked who you were."

The caller stammered around not knowing how to respond and finally said, "Well I don't want to get in trouble."

"Then answer my question."

More stammering then, "Well, my name's Billy."

"I thought so," Mike replied, "Allan told me about you."

"Well I know some important stuff and I don't just blab it to everyone. I just wanted to make sure you were the right guy."

"You got the right guy alright, but I don't want to discuss it over the phone. Can you meet me tomorrow night?"

"What's in it for me?"

"A couple of beers for starters," Mike said as he thought to himself, this guy will be a pushover. *He's just bursting to spill his guts.*

Chapter Twenty-three

Billy

Billy fumbled with the key, finally found the slot, and entered his new double wide trailer. He and his wife Mary Lou purchased it a few months ago after he had finally settled down and managed to keep a steady job for almost a year now. She had always worked and supported them through the lean years when he jumped from job to job. He was always quitting because the foreman was getting on his ass, or getting fed up with hard work, or getting fired for various reasons.

Tonight was no exception to his usual routine. He would come home after Mary Lou was in bed and wake her up with his beer breath wanting either sex or conversation. As Allan said, Billy was a talker and when his brain was stimulated with anything slightly out of the ordinary, it gave him fuel to burn. Tonight it was conversation he was seeking. Mary Lou was used to it and somehow took all this in stride. With all his faults she loved him dearly. They had been high school sweethearts and married soon after graduation. It was with sleepy reluctance she rolled over and answered Billy's insistent murmuring,

"Lou, Mary Lou, wake up."

"What is it Billy?"

"I got some important news."

"What is it, Billy?"

"you know that guy you been talking about. The guy I did that paint job for, on his airboat."

"You mean Orin Taylor?"

"There's this guy that's investigatin' that Orin fellow."

"What do you mean Billy? You haven't been repeating what I been telling you have you?"

"Well, not exactly."

"Billy," she remarked with a touch of anger in her voice. She knew how Billy loved to talk especially if the talk could inflate his ego, "You know that could get me fired."

"No way. Hell, you ought to quit that job anyway. You know it's a dead end street. You been working for that tightwad crook too damn long as it is."

Her long time role as the major bread winner was entrenched in her psyche. In the back of her mind she kept the fear that Billy would come home early some day with his final check in his hand and she would be back in her supportive role once more. She had wanted to quit this job many times but now that they could actually afford for her to be out of work, she couldn't accept the idea of it. The thought of getting fired threatened her very existence. On the other hand she often thought of looking for another job. She had never liked Bobby Duncan and she knew he was up to something crooked in that store and it scared her. This was what she and Billy had had numerous conversations about. "It just scares me to think about him finding out we've been talking about him behind his back."

"It ought to scare *him* more'n you."

"Who's this guy that's investigating him?"

"He ain't investigatin' Bobby, he's investigatin' that Orin fellow. His name is Mike and I think he's working under cover for some big organization like the IRS or FBI. I'm supposed to meet him tomorrow night at Hooters up in Ocala."

"Billy, don't tell him anything," she pleaded.

"Allan says this Mike would make it worth my while, meaning he will pay for any information I give him."

"Billy, please don't get involved."

"Look, Lou let's face it, if Bobby is involved in somethin' crooked and you work for him, you are already involved."

"Maybe, but I haven't done anything wrong."

"Yeah, but you have to let them know that before they start investigatin' you too."

"Do you think they will?"

"It sounds like they're on to something, and it has to do with that Orin fellow. It's got to be his connection with Bobby Duncan."

"Oh, Billy," she said with tears in her eyes, "I'm scared."

"Look at it this way. If you tell them what you know, they'll likely give you a medal instead of puttin' you in jail. They'll know you ain't done nothin'."

"I guess so. It's just scary that's all."

They talked for another hour and then Billy made love to her and calmed her to where sleep was once again possible. She slept not knowing what torment she would struggle with as she faced the man she worked for in the next few days. To betray someone, even on the side of right instills a sense of wrong-doing in the righteous.

Chapter Twenty-four

Here's the deal

Mike could tell it was Billy when he first saw him enter Hooters and look around. He recognized him from his Florida Gators hat and clandestine actions. This guy was a real piece of work. Hooters was far enough out of Orin's and Bobby's territory that chances of one of them wandering in while he and Billy were talking was slim to none. They didn't know Mike but it was essential that they didn't know he had a connection with Billy. Mike had left his name with the hostess and told her someone would be joining him. He saw them both look his way and caught the second look the hostess gave Billy as he walked towards his booth. At this point Billy had looked over his shoulder at least four times. As he sat down Mike extended his hand and introduced himself and Billy looked over his shoulder again and said, "Hi." then whispered, "I'm Billy."

Mike smiled and said, "Billy, you need to relax. There is no one in this building who gives a shit about you and me or the conversation we are about to have."

Billy puffed himself up and said, "You can't be too careful in this business."

Mike looked at him without the smile and asked, "What business is that, Billy?"

"Well, you know," he stammered, "this," and he looked over his shoulder and whispered, "investigation."

"Billy, as I said in the beginning, relax. Let's have a beer. You want some wings?"

"Sure," Billy said and puffed up again, "I like 'em hot."

Mike ordered and Billy started to calm down a little after the first beer. They engaged in small talk about Billy's job and

Mary Lou's position with Bobby's company, and then Mike asked, "What did Allan tell you about me?"

"Nothing, uh, I mean not much. He said you were looking for information on Orin Taylor. He said you would make it worth my while," he said as his eyes shifted over the customers at the bar.

"Are you enjoying your beer and wings?" Mike asked with his dark eyes boring holes in Billy.

"Well I ain't telling you nothing for just some beer and chicken wings," Billy stated defiantly.

"Oh, I think you will and I may even want to ask your wife a few questions, now that I know she is involved. That is, unless you tell me everything I need to know."

Billy pulled his hat off his head and wiped some sweat off his forehead put his hat back on and looked hard at Mike.

"What's the matter Billy, your wings too hot?"

"What do you want from me?" Billy said as he dropped his eyes, unable to match Mike's steady gaze. "Who are you with? Who the hell are you?"

"Look, Billy, who I am and who I am with is not important. What I want from you is important. You are going to tell me everything you know about Orin Taylor and his relationship with Bobby Duncan. What you get out of it is a few beers, a few hot wings and peace of mind for you and your wife. Someone more important than me will know you and your wife are cooperating in this, and that will be worth a great deal to your wife. Now my first question is this;" a long pause for effect then, "are you cooperating?" and the cold dark stare bore on, waiting for an answer.

The silence was oppressive as Billy still stared at the table, not moving, a half a chicken wing dangling from his fingers. Mike enjoyed the power he held over Billy and decided to use it to its fullest. With Billy's notion that Mike was some kind of undercover agent, it opened doors that would be locked tight otherwise.

Billy finally looked up and met the icy stare. "Ok," he mumbled under his breath, "I'll cooperate."

"Good, now have another beer and we'll start over."

Just like Mike knew he would, Billy spilled his guts. And when he finished he pleaded with Mike not to question Mary Lou.

Mike said he didn't think he would have to. Billy was a lot smarter than he appeared and was well informed from Mary Lou. Mike thought he knew exactly what was going on between Orin and Bobby. A plan to find out for sure started to form in his head. He wanted Mary Lou to arrange something for him. After Mike told him what it was, Billy agreed to ask her but made no promises. Mike grinned and said, "She'll do it; she doesn't have a choice."

Chapter Twenty-five

The pecking order

Orin sat at his desk in the mobile construction office, his head on his arms. The throbbing continued despite the aspirin. It was early afternoon and his hangover was still there. He knew a stiff drink or two would take away the pain but he didn't want to dull his senses before his meeting with Bobby. There would be time for a drink after their meeting. If things went well Bobby would have a drink with him. He was thankful this was a Saturday. The phone wouldn't ring with those dumb-ass questions from Tom. "Would the Uke be running next week?" "What would it cost?" "Can we just patch it up?" His respect for Tom had disappeared long ago.

Tom Mathis was a self made man and had built Mathis Construction to a multi-million dollar company with big contracts over a five county area. Tom's strength was in sales and knowing how to bid the jobs, he depended on his job foremen to get the jobs done and he had some good foremen. But Tom's ability to keep his company on the move went right over Orin's head. Orin assumed the jobs just fell out of the sky and he had no idea of the work, research and planning it took to land a big job. Tom's dedication to this end of the business left him with little time to oversee Orin's job and this apathy had allowed Orin to take advantage. He had started cheating Tom long ago. It started with falsifying hours and graduated to just plain thievery of parts, diesel fuel, any materials he could get his hands on without Tom's knowledge. He thought of Tom as stupid instead of trusting, as naive instead of generous. When Tom would release leftover material for him to dispose of, Orin would nearly always come out with something in his own pocket while laughing at what Orin mistook as Tom's ignorance.

Orin's greed and his ability to spend money before he made it, led him to his unholy alliance with Bobby Duncan. He needed a steadier income instead of the dribbles from these spontaneous opportunities, which sometimes involved a certain amount of work. He knew he could persuade Bobby, force him to go along.

Bobby, although physically much larger than Orin, had always given in to him. This came from their teenage years when Orin grew in size faster and was more mature. They went through high school together with Orin calling the shots and Bobby who was smarter and eventually much bigger just tagging along until they parted right after high school. Bobby went on to college in Gainesville and Orin hired on as a mechanic with a construction company. The two crossed paths years later when Bobby moved back to Ocala to open a parts store with his dad's backing. The store specialized in parts for heavy machinery and catered to the construction business. Orin, who was in charge of maintenance for Tom Mathis started buying his supplies and parts from Bobby. He soon figured out how to turn this into a source of steady income for his drinking and gambling habits. Bobby had been a reluctant and fearful participant who succumbed to Orin's persuasive urgings. It had started with a few small items and escalated into a nice sideline for Orin, and a nice cushion for Bobby in the throes of getting his new business started. Bobby wanted out now and kept trying to convince Orin to quit their scam.

It had been a month since their last meeting and Orin once again would have to threaten Bobby and coerce him into continuing their alliance. He knew Bobby had no choice but to continue, just as he knew he would never get caught. Their arrangement incriminated Bobby to a much greater degree than Orin, and that was the hold he had over Bobby. They saw each other sometimes on a daily basis but both had sworn not to talk business—their secret business—except when they were alone with little chance of interruption. When Orin new they would have a heated discussion, as he knew they would today, he would meet him at one of their remote construction sites—on a weekend when the crews weren't working. Tom never visited these sites on the weekend unless the crews were working. They sometimes took an airboat ride or met at The Crossroads if a problem needed resolving quickly, but these deserted sites made a better atmosphere for coercion. Bobby generally drove his company pickup instead of his street rod, in case Tom or one of the foremen came by. It would look like business instead of personal.

Tom Mathis had no idea how personal their meetings really were, or how much those meetings meant to him personally. If he knew how often they were meeting he would start to worry. Tom trusted Orin and left him to his own resources except in emergencies or when they were pushing for a deadline that would cost him money. In that respect Orin earned his money and most of the time came through for Tom.

Orin had dozed off when Bobby's knock startled him awake. The booze from the night before still had its hold on him. He let him in and opened the shades on the windows facing the only road in and they sat looking at each other with blank faces.

"You look like shit," Bobby said with a trace of disgust in his voice.

"I had a rough night."

"You have several of those each week and I think they're getting more frequent."

"Screw you."

"Look Orin, that's one of the things that bothers me about our deal."

"What's that Bobby?"

"You getting shit-faced every night. You're not stable anymore. You don't know what you'll say to someone someday. Both our asses will be in slings with the IRS if you blab to the wrong person."

"Bobby," and Orin looked at him with the dominate stare that had cowed Bobby hundreds of times before, "you know I haven't told anyone and you know I won't tell anyone. Now tell me what this is really about."

"You know what it's about, I'm scared. We are bound to get caught if we keep this up." Bobby tried to assert himself but Orin wasn't buying it. They discussed it for another half hour with the result that Bobby had no specific reason for getting jittery. Just the same old bullshit that Orin had heard over and over. Orin finally calmed him down with promises that they could start easing up and wind the scam down at the end of this year, reminding him that if they quit suddenly it could raise a flag with the parts expenditures dropping too quickly without apparent reason. Even if Tom Mathis was stupid, his bookkeeper was not.

"Let's go get a drink at The Crossroads and shoot a game of pool?" Orin smiled knowing he had won another battle.

"OK, but I only have time for a short one, Brenda's wants me to take her out tonight. Oh, I almost forgot, Mary Lou said her husband—you know . . . Billy Cravens, the guy who painted your boat—heard of a fellow who was a good pool player and thought you two ought to square off. Are you game, or better yet, can you stay sober long enough to play a whole game of pool?"

"I don't need to be sober to beat your ass at anything. Sure," Orin said, always ready for a good game of pool, "I'll take him on. What's his name?"

"Mike something. I'll find out from Mary Lou, and make the arrangements."

Chapter Twenty-six

Play the game

Orin felt good tonight. He hadn't felt this good for a long time, exactly five years. He had had a couple of beers, but for Orin, that was just a start. He usually had a couple of beers and started thinking and that led to the hard stuff. His thoughts were usually centered around Betty, his ex wife and the night she left him. The only problem being that he hadn't seen Betty for five years. He knew that Betty was the best thing that had ever happened to him and that she would never come back. He had driven her away. This was his greatest loss. He had not seen Betty since that horrible night. He knew why she had left him and even where she was now, but he also knew she would not come back. He knew, but couldn't accept.

Tonight was different. He had a new girlfriend and thought she was about ready to move in with him. He was inflated by his ego; things seemed to be going better of late: the girl really seemed to like him, Bobby was back on track, and his reputation as a pool player had gotten him this match with one of the best players around—if this Billy Cravens could be believed. Orin was, generally speaking, a good pool player, but this challenger was supposed to be the best according to Billy and Allan. He was to meet him tonight at the Crossroads. It was an arranged match in that several interested individuals had encouraged it. The bartender Allan knew this guy and mentioned it to Billy Cravens who got the word to Bobby. At least that's what Orin and Bobby thought.

Orin, being gifted in the game of pool, could hold his own even when his alcohol consumption exceeded his capacity. He had never heard of his challenger, but knew that he must be a formidable player or his buddies would have never suggested this meeting take place. There would be a lot of money change hands, but most of it would not go to the players. They were involved to the extent of their reputations. Their bet, although substantial, was miniscule in comparison to the total of the side bets. If this does not seem fair, it is of no consequence. It was totally fair to the participants. Their reputations were at stake and they would do their best to protect them.

The Game was eight ball and the first set was paid for by whoever lost the toss, fifty cents down the drain for the loser, who also had to rack the balls. The winner got to break and this was usually an advantage, for if he got a good break and put a ball or two in, then he might be able to run the table, sink the eight ball and win the game. But if he missed the break and left a good shot for his opponent, the tables could be reversed. The opponent could run the table and sink the eight ball and win the game. This is all under the assumption that the challenger and the challenged could run the table. This was not often the case. Someone would miss and the next player would get his chance. The introductions came over a beer and the two players and their friends got acquainted.

Orin was as sober as he ever was at this time of day. He had eaten his dinner right here from the hors d'oeuvres that the Crossroads offered every Friday night, while his opponent, had arrived with a full dinner under his belt and a mission to accomplish. Orin won the break and proceeded to run the table up to his last ball before the eight, and missed the bank shot. Mike then ran all his balls and dropped the eight for the victory. The shots were routine and no one was overly impressed. Mike broke for the next game and sunk a stripe, ran three balls and had a difficult bank shot to continue. He missed and Orin took over, ran the rest of the solids and sunk the eight. At this point the match was all even and the real purpose of this contest was not yet disclosed.

It was Orin's break; he had a good one and ran the table for his second win. It was Orin's break again and this time the break left him stymied and Orin attempted to hide the cue ball, since he didn't have a decent shot at his own balls.

Mike thought, that shows a weakness in character. This guys a wimp. He had a tough shot, but this is the chicken way out. "Nice leave," Mike said with a devilish grin. The gallery was chuckling. Mike could have done the same thing to Orin, for his shot was even more difficult than Orin's had been. He could bury the cue ball where Orin had no shot at all, but it wasn't in his nature. He had to win this game or lose the match. They were playing best three out of five games wins the match. He thought he could make this shot and if he did it would set the stage for what he had in mind for Orin. He didn't need to win but it would help. He called the seven in the corner, cued the ball low and struck it firmly. The cue ball jumped over the eleven careened off the rail barely bumping the seven which was hanging near the corner pocket. It dropped with a soft thump as the gallery hooted; "Damn, what a shot. Hell of a shot, Mike." Orin stood still with an angry look on his face.

Mike went on to win this set which made them all even going into the final game and Orin racked them for Mike as was the custom. Instead of breaking, Mike walked to the racked balls and looked hard at the balls and then at Orin. "Would you like to rack them again?" he said with an icy stare.

Orin's face turned beet red as he flustered and muttered, "What's the matter?"

"I'd like a tight rack." said Mike continuing to stare at Orin. He had seen Orin use his fingers to slightly separate the balls. A lose rack could result in a poor break and a chance for Orin to run the table for a win.

Orin began to wilt under Mike's dark stare and tried to make light of the situation while reaching for the rack. He racked them under Mike's watchful eye and when he was finished, said, "Does that suit you?"

Mike didn't say a word but walked to the other end of the table and lined up for the break. He had a good break with a solid falling and ran two more before missing a difficult shot. Orin ran three straight and Mike turned to the waitress to order a round of beers as Orin lined up and shot for the fourth time. The nine ball headed for the side pocket and hit the rail on the near side and rolled slowly to the corner and plunked in as Mike was returning his attention back to the game. "Did you call that shot?" Mike asked. "It looked to me like you were going to shoot for the side pocket."

"Sure I called it. . . . Ask Bobby," Orin said as he glared at Bobby whose face was turning red.

"What about it, Bobby, did he call it in the corner?"

"I saw him wave his cue that way," Bobby said sheepishly and regretted his words as soon as they left his mouth. *Why am I covering for that bastard?* He's good enough to win without cheating but he just has to do it, he thought to himself.

Mike knew he was lying and thought, *this is working out great.* Mike saw Randy Nolan looking on with his mouth hanging open. Randy who was a friend of Allan's knew Mike and had seen him shoot several times before. Mike knew Randy was about to offer his opinion when Mike caught his eye and winked and shook his head sideways. Mike thought, *Randy must have some money on me.* Randy's mouth closed with a puzzled look on his face.

Orin ran the other three balls and sunk the eight ball with a big grin on his face; the match was his. Mike longed to wipe off that grin, but there were more important things to do. He could tell by the disappointed looks on most of the faces that he had been favored to win. Under other circumstances he would not have let Orin get away with that slop shot, but he thought he could use it to his advantage. He would like to have won, he could still have used that to his advantage, but this will work out even better. Orin was indeed a good player even if he did have some character flaws.

He walked to Orin, put out his hand, and said, "Good match Orin, can I buy you and your friend a beer?" motioning at Bobby.

"Sure," said Orin, "let's set at a table. C'mon Bobby."

They moved towards a table and Mike motioned for Randy to join them and Randy declined, indicating he would rather sit with someone else. Mike wasn't sure whether it was him or Orin that Randy didn't want to sit beside. Mike was sure Randy knew that Mike had let the slop shot go on purpose and it had probably cost him a good sum of money. Mike knew he hadn't heard the end of this. He would have to make it up to Randy and explain someday.

The three of them drank beer and talked pool while Mike studied Orin and Bobby trying to determine the depth of their relationship. Mike approached the subject with a question, "You two work together?"

"Naw," said Bobby, "I run a little parts place near Ocala and Orin here buys some parts from us."

"What do you do, Orin?" Mike asked.

"I'm the maintenance foreman for a construction company . . . Mathis Construction up in Ocala."

"Yeah," Mike said, "I've heard of them. Big outfit. Must keep you pretty busy. You must buy a lot of parts from Bobby." It was said as a statement not a question and drew no answer just a sideways glance between the two. They finished their beers and Mike decided he couldn't get close to Orin in a hundred years. There was nothing about the man that he liked or could even identify with for that matter. He felt there was some kind of bond between Orin and Bobby and felt like it was not necessarily friendship that held them together. He suspected that Orin had some hold on Bobby and he had an idea what it was. Bobby's mistake of backing up Orin's lie at the pool table would soon come back to haunt him. He would know their secret, and figure out how to use it before long.

Mike stood as if to leave and they stood with him. Mike excused himself and said to Bobby, "Allan said you have a 32 Ford roadster street rod. Come outside, I want to show you something." He put his arm around Bobby, turned his back to Orin, excluding him from the invitation, and started Bobby towards the door. Orin was too full of himself for winning to let it bother him and walked towards the bar.

Bobby was a good sized country boy but showed no resistance as Mike led him out the door. Mike had parked around back for two reasons. One was to prevent some drunk from scratching his pickup and to prepare for this meeting with someone and it happened to be Bobby.

95

Chapter Twenty-seven

To tell the truth . . .

Mike started telling him about his Chevy as they were walking and Bobby was a good listener. He seemed genuinely interested and asked Mike to raise the hood, which he did. Mike stepped to the side to give himself a view of the side parking lot. He wanted to make sure that Orin hadn't followed them. He didn't need a witness to what he was about to do. If someone came up later he could explain it away, but not if they saw the whole thing. Mike turned towards Bobby and said, "You're not going to like this," and punched him in the gut, hard enough to knock the wind out of him.

Mike hit him a little harder than he intended to and almost knocked him out. Bobby staggered against the fender of the pickup gasping for breath but maintained his balance. He was bent over with his arms on his stomach. His legs were bent and his feet wide apart. He looked like he was on his way down and out, but Mike had been here before and saw what was coming. Bobby's right hand dropped to his side and he continued to gasp but Mike saw his weight shift slightly to his right leg. When the blow came Mike was ready for it. Bobby brought it up from the cellar and if it had connected, it might have torn Mike's head off. But Mike knew it would come to his head and dropped just under it while delivering another shot to Bobby's solar plexus. This time Bobby went down to his knees and Mike knew the fight would be out of him. Bobby fell forward catching himself with his extended arms and stayed there on his hands and knees while disgorging his last meal and three hours of Beer into the gravel.

Bobby's breath finally came back and he whispered, "Goddamn, what was that for?" still on his hands and knees.

"I should have done it to Orin for claiming he called that slop shot, but you shouldn't have backed him up. You see, I am a vengeful kind of guy and you're going to help me get revenge, a little from you and a lot from Orin. You have something I need and I think this will help me get it. I am going to ask you a few simple questions and you will answer them truthfully. Some of them will be easy and I could get them elsewhere but this will be quicker. Some of them I already know the answers to, so you best be truthful."

"I'm not answering any of your Goddamn questions." Bobby's wind and courage obviously built as he regained his feet.

"You will unless you want to go down with Orin." Mike said with his dark eyes and sinister grin boring into Bobby's treasure house of guilt. "The punches were just to get your attention, with a little payback attached. We can carry that part a little further if you like or we can get down to business. That is unless you want to keep protecting Orin while he laughs at you."

"What the hell?" Bobby said, "Who are you? What the hell you want from me?"

Mike could tell he had struck a nerve with more than his punches. Bobby broke out in a sweat. Mike knew he had left him no choice but to listen, his guilt would not let him do otherwise. Mike imagined the fear of discovery Bobby harbored over his dealings with Orin, and could see that fear consume him. Like in his meeting with Billy, Mike's leverage grew out of their own fears, guilt, and assumptions.

Mike, armed with the information supplied by Mary Lou through Billy, knew exactly which questions to ask. He asked a few questions which Bobby didn't answer but Mike knew he had Bobby's attention and that the fight was over. Mike was sure that Bobby thought he was connected with some unknown authority, and Mike's line of questioning and the extent of his knowledge bore that out. His questions proved that he knew Bobby's business, and implied that he was a part of some big investigation—the IRS probably, or maybe some unrelated thing with Orin.

He began to answer reluctantly when Mike assured him it was Orin who was really on the hot seat and that Bobby ought to choose sides right now. "Which will it be? Work with me or Orin?"

Bobby told Mike that he had been living with the threat of getting caught ever since Orin had approached him with his scheme. Orin was in charge of maintenance for Mathis Construction and bought all parts from Bobby's company. Orin allowed Bobby to charge Mathis retail for the parts and Orin would put his O.K. on all the bills. Tom Mathis trusted Orin as his long time employee and never questioned that Orin wasn't getting the fleet discounts that most large scale buyers get on parts. Bobby was making a killing, but Orin was there with his hand out wanting half of all the excess profit, and Orin kept his own set of books at home to make sure he got his fair share—in cash. Bobby had discovered this when he inadvertently shortchanged Orin one time. Orin put a stop to that and when Bobby wanted to quit, Orin threatened to disclose it as Bobby's scam, saying that he just discovered it.

Bobby said, "Hell, he really had me over a barrel, since the first dirty money passed over the counter." Said he didn't have anything on Orin. All Orin's money had been cash under the counter and Bobby had had to do some financial footwork to cover those expenditures. The fancy footwork held up with his accountant, but may not pass the rigid scrutiny of any investigation if it came to that. The authorities would just think he had stashed the cash as untaxed fun money. Some of the payoffs came out of his earnings, which he paid taxes on, while Orin wallowed in untraceable cash.

"How could I have been so stupid?" Bobby lamented.

Mike agreed with him. Mike finally had sufficient information on that subject; he knew or suspected most of it from Billy's conversation. Bobby assured him that he would keep his mouth shut around Orin about being questioned. He could see that Orin had Bobby by the balls, and he thought that Bobby had sense enough to know that he needed to co-operate with any investigation into this matter. Mike knew he wouldn't tell Orin about this meeting.

This hadn't turned out the way Mike had planned it. He wasn't sure he had enough to force Orin's hand in the way he wanted to. Orin had skillfully kept himself out of the traceable loop. Sure, the IRS could bring them both down in time and he would see that they had a good start after he got what he wanted.

But he thought he may need another approach to getting what he wanted out of Mr. Orin Taylor.

Mike started a new line of questions, which seemed to befuddle Bobby. An investigation of any size would already have the answers to the questions Mike was asking, but Mike hoped Bobby would think he designed the questions to check his answers. He wanted Bobby to think they were after Orin as much or more than him, anyway.

"I heard Orin has a new girl friend. I want her name and address." and Mike's dark eyes bore into Bobby's eyes searching for truth. He got his answer and found she lived on the Withlacoochee down near Dunnellon and that Orin was seeing her every weekend. He continued and found that Orin lived alone, drank too much almost every night, he usually went to see his girlfriend Kathy in his airboat. She lived down the river from Orin. His airboat was named *Wet Dream*. He said that Orin was trying to get her to move in with him but he thought she had better sense and didn't care that much for him. She was rather homely but had a nice personality and could do a lot better than Orin. No, Orin had no close friends. He had no children, at least that he ever spoke of. Mike learned about Orin's daily habits: when he got home from work, on what nights, his favorite watering holes, and when he would be likely to go there. Orin had been married to a woman named Betty until about five years ago, and when she left, was when he really went off the deep end. He drank himself into a stupor most every night. He nearly lost his job. The new girls he would meet didn't seem to last long. Yes, he was a violent person when he got riled and the first time he showed that side of him the girl usually broke it off.

Mike got all the information he needed and then some. He now had a hold on Orin. Bobby had opened up as if someone had released a flood gate. He was getting it all off his chest as if glad to be telling someone, and if he had to face up to jail, he would. Mike made sure Bobby wouldn't tell Orin by telling Bobby that he would see to it that when it came down, he would get special consideration, if he didn't warn Orin. He asked Bobby to go on with the scam as if nothing had happened, or until he heard otherwise. Mike had an idea that Bobby was just about ready to stand up against Orin, but it just may be too late.

Chapter Twenty-eight

Plan your work, then work your plan

Mike had learned Orin's habits well. The key was being sure when he would be coming and sure that he would be alone. The first part was the easiest because Orin usually visited his girlfriend every Friday night and it was of course always preceded by the trip downriver. He needed to set up a watch somewhere between Orin's house and hers. He could do this himself but he would need some way to make sure it was Orin and that he was alone. Mike would love to have some help to pull this off but he knew he had to go it alone. He didn't want anyone else involved. Someone else could get squeamish and back out or run off at the mouth bragging about it if it went well. He knew he could trust Jim on all counts but he didn't want to put Jim at risk. The less Jim or anyone else knew about this the better off he was. He just had to figure it out and eliminate the chance for mistakes.

When it came, it was a simple plan as all good plans are. He went over and over it in his mind and gave it 100 to 1 odds of succeeding. *Pretty good odds, he thought, if you're not betting your life.* But he was. He had a few loose ends, and if everything checked out like he thought, he would be ready next Friday. Without help he would have to take a chance on Orin sticking to his regular Friday night habits. His plan had some fail safe features if something went wrong, and the worst case scenario seemed to be just thirty hours of his time wasted if it didn't work.

Friday came and Mike was having his usual day right up to about noon. He went into Stumpys for a bite to eat and quick beer. The Bartender was Freddy, and he commented on the beer, knowing Mike usually didn't drink in the middle of the day, which was just what Mike wanted him to do. "I'm taking off for a couple of days," Mike replied to Freddy's comment about the beer.

"Where you goin'?" Freddy asked.

"I'm going over to Stuart and see an old friend I haven't seen for a few years. He's working on a research ship out of Woods Hole and he'll be laid up in Stuart for a few days. I'll be back sometime late tomorrow. Keep an eye on my boat for me, OK?"

"Sure, Mike, I'll check it when I leave tonight and when I come in tomorrow morning."

"Thanks Fred. I'll take you fishing someday."

Mike finished his lunch and declined the second beer with, "No, I got a long drive ahead of me and two beers will make me sleepy." Mike started up his Chevy truck and drove south down Highway 200, the well tuned v8 humming like a bass violin. He made Stuart in four hours, checked into the Harbor Inn on North River Drive and made a phone call. Twenty minutes later Kurt Daggot met him in the parking lot. They had a brief conversation and then each of them drove off, Mike in Kurt's rental Dodge and Kurt in Mike's pickup.

Four hours later Mike was in Dunnellon across the street from Anglers Fishing Headquarters in the parking lot of the public boat ramp. He waited until sure Anglers was closed and all the lingerers had gone. Most of the boats were in and the dock was deserted. Mike kept his second boat here for fishing trips, it was closer to Lake Rousseau, and he used his boat at Stumpknockers strictly for sightseeing. This boat was smaller and older. He didn't mind the wear and tear it got from his fishing clients. He wanted to keep his newer boat clean. He parked at the public boat ramp across the street where the night fishermen parked. He figured one more car wouldn't be noticed. He backed it into the corner so no one could see the out-of-county-license without making a special effort. He waited until the street was clear and crossed quickly.

His boat was in the far end slip and it would be hard to tell it was gone even if someone was looking for it. He quietly took off the cover, started the motor without revving it up, and let it idle while he untied the lines. He eased out into the current, letting the stern swing downstream, gave it a just little throttle and headed up stream. He figured he had about an hour to kill, but he still had some things to do. A good distance from the dock he revved her up on plane, turned on his running lights and laid his spotlight next to the console where he could reach it quickly. He slowed for the first rapid and worked his way through. There were no exposed rocks but several were just below the surface. He knew how to read the water in the daylight and avoid a bent prop or broken shear pin, but this was different. He hit the tilt to raise the motor as much as he could and still make headway against the current. Then strictly by memory, using some unique tree as a guide, he would take one heading and then another, when two trees lined up or a certain stump came into view. He throttled up again and drove on up the river repeating the same procedure at the next rapid.

He arrived just short of Orin's girlfriend's house about ten o'clock and slowed to a creep as he approached with his lights off. He idled into a cove about a hundred yards from her dock. He took out his binoculars and scanned the dock. *Yes!* There was Orin's airboat, *Wet Dream*, the name written bold on the tail fin. *So far so good.* There was an eerie light around the dock area. *Tiki lights? Haven't seen those in a while. Are they sitting outside? Or maybe on the porch?* They were probably on the Porch, otherwise the mosquitoes would run them inside. He knew there were dogs in the neighborhood. He couldn't risk walking the bank. The underbrush was too thick for silent walking anyway. He knew what he would have to do and knew the risk involved. No one in their right mind would swim at night in the Withlacoochee River. He would take his light but wouldn't use it unless he had to. *Would the light scare a gator?* He didn't think so. They say a gator will relax its jaws if you bang it on the snout real hard but he saw them try to demonstrate that at a gator farm one time and they must have had a stubborn gator. He held on tight. Well, if the light wouldn't scare him, and he couldn't hit him hard enough, he still had his dive knife. *Hell, here I am psyching myself out.*

He slipped into his wet suit, added an extra weight to his weight belt and put it on, clipped on his dive light tether, strapped on his depth gage and pulled on his fins. He laid his mask on the deck and quietly slid into the water. He didn't use a snorkel; someone on shore would hear it blow when he cleared it. He adjusted his mask, rubbed some spit in it to clear the fog, took a deep breath and let himself sink to the bottom. He silently stroked his way along the shoreline staying at the same depth along the bottom. Visibility was zero from the lack of light but the water was clear enough for him to read the luminous dial on his depth gage. He came up for a breath and cautiously exhaled and inhaled a few times while looking around. He was doing quite well. He took another deep breath and dropped to the bottom again. By staying at the same depth he would not drift out into the center of the river or circle into the bank. He saw it was working as he came up for another breath. He was almost there. This time he breast stroked smoothly up under the dock and stood there in the shallow water next to *Wet Dream* with just his head out of the water. His every move was slow and cautious; he could not afford to be discovered here.

He let his unused dive light dangle and took a small rope about three feet long from under his weight belt. It had a screwdriver tied to one end. He silently worked his way to the stern end of *Wet Dream* and slowly stood up keeping the bulk of the boat and its huge motor between him and the house. He could hear them talking in low tones. *Damn, they must be out in the yard.* He knew then he had to be extra quiet. He reached over the transom and used the screwdriver to loosen the clamp on the gas line from the tank to the fuel pump. Then he tied the line he brought to the transom plug which was a standard quick release plug. He led the line up and over the loosened gas line and coiled the remainder up and stuffed it under the edge of the tank.

He pulled his wet suit hood back from his ears and tried to make out what they were saying. He could tell they were not far away but he couldn't see them. They were having a low keyed argument. She was telling him why she couldn't or wouldn't move in with him and he was trying to convince her otherwise with the thick tongue of one too many beers. He was pathetic. Mike now had a sense of urgency as he thought: What if he gets mad and leaves before I'm ready? What if she throws him out early? All this will be wasted! He took a mighty breath of air, ducked under and stroked back the way he came. He was there in two breaths and as he silently pulled himself onto the deck he realized he hadn't thought about a gator through the whole thing. He had left his boat quietly idling while he was gone, to supply him with a quick getaway if he needed it, and to eliminate the sound of the starter motor when he returned. He eased the boat back into the river and drifted around the bend a quarter of a mile downstream, where he turned on the running lights, headed back upstream and goosed her up on plane. He passed *Wet Dream* still at the dock and started to breathe again. *It was going good.* He drove up to the spot he had scouted out the day before, where the river narrowed to the point where it would be hard to pass on either side. The current was slow here and it was deep, a good place to fish. He dropped the anchor, got out his fishing rod and started fishing for catfish.

Chapter Twenty-nine

Homeward bound

Orin was pissed off and had the throttle of his airboat over halfway open. *This girl is just leadin' me on. Where does she come off with that shit about my drinkin'? Hell, I can hold my liquor. I'm tired of livin' alone. I've been treatin' her like a queen.*

He'd left in a spray of wind and water. He hoped she was still standing near the dock. It felt good to really get on it. He had made this trip at least twice a week for the last few weeks and knew every rock in the river, at least the ones he had to avoid. He left his running lights off as he often did. They impaired his vision at night and he figured it was more important for him to see than for someone to see him. Beside he knew they could hear him long before they would see his lights if he had them on. It never occurred to him that some other fool in another airboat might be thinking exactly the same thing. He was fortunate there weren't too many boaters who thought like him.

It was dark tonight but the sheen off the water and the darker forms of the trees told him where to go. He had his goggles and earmuffs on, guarding against the night bugs and dangerous noise of the unmuffled engine. He enjoyed running at night more than the day. It was cool, but he had his windbreaker on and didn't mind it. He smiled to himself as he passed the tree with the eagle's nest. That nest hadn't been there but a couple of years. He had planted a bush under that tree five years ago, and no one had discovered what was under that bush. Planting that bush was the only smart thing he had done that night. That's what made him smile each time he passed that tree.

He was clever to have put that bush there; it didn't take long for the area to return to a natural look. Now no one would ever know and even if they did there was no connection to him. He had kept his little secrets all to himself these five years. He had not told a soul even though at times he longed to do so. He had felt the same need for speed that night that he did now. That night remained vivid in his memory . . .

———————

Orin gave *Wet Dream* full throttle as he left Blue Spring that evening five years ago, the blast of air and water from the whirling prop, leaving all behind him in a damp cloud. He turned the boat downstream with a vengeance. *I'll show that bitch. She can't humiliate me like that. I'll show that Goddamn Charlie too, next time I see him.* These angry thoughts filled his alcohol soaked brain, the calming force of speeding in his airboat, had not yet taken affect. The alcohol had numbed his senses, and he didn't see the sharp turn coming up, but it wouldn't have made any difference; he was going too fast to make it on the correct line. It was not until he saw the tree and the boy in the fishing boat that he knew he had waited too late to start the turn. He pulled the stick hard right in an attempt to miss the boy. An airboat will slide through a turn and even turn completely around and be off in the opposite direction with the right person at the stick. Six beers and a heart full of anger had slowed his reaction time to less than the required level to make such a maneuver under control, at least not without dire consequences. That he didn't turn *Wet Dream* over or swamp her out was a miracle, a miracle with drastic results.

He didn't hear the boy holler through the scream of his engine. He didn't see the huge wake of his airboat swamp the little fishing boat. He didn't see the struggling boy get blown overboard as the airboat swapped ends and directed a stream of fierce prop-wash directly at the fragile little craft. His boat swung a deadly arc as it blew the remaining dead leaves off the downed cypress the small boat was tied to. The screaming roar of the engine was reduced to a soft throb as Orin released the throttle and allowed his dull senses to catch up. He cut the engine and the powerless airboat drifted with the current and lodged into the outer branches of the tree near where the fishing boat lay swamped and sinking. The boy was struggling to get back in the sinking boat, shouting something, but Orin couldn't hear him. Orin finally saw the boy was in trouble. The adrenalin was overtaking the alcohol as his heart beat pounded in his ears. He realized he still had his earmuffs on and tore them off, tossing them towards the pilot's seat, as he lunged to grab the same limb the boy's boat was up against. He extended his arm out to the boy who was struggling hard to reach for the same limb. Their arms met and they locked wrists. The boy was coughing now instead of shouting. His grip was weak and his arm slippery. Something was dragging the boy under as it sunk deeper in the water. Orin pulled with desperate strength to keep the boy's head above the water. The boy's loose grip soon relaxed completely. Orin's own grip began to loosen and the boy's limp hand slipped through his. He watched the boy sink further beneath the water and he realized he had something in his hand.

As the boy's body sank out of sight still captured by some unseen force beneath the black water, waves of revulsion wracked Orin's body. "Oh, God, what have I done?" he sobbed out loud. He lay exhausted, clutching the boy's watch to his breast. The tremendous weight of guilt held him against the side of the boat for what seemed like an hour but in reality was only a few minutes. As he slowly became aware that he had to do something, to get help, to tell someone, his thoughts turned to Betty back at the spring. She was getting a ride home with Charlie and his family; they were already in the car when he left the spring. He thrust the boy's watch in his pocket, pushed the idling boat out in the current, and rushed to the controls. He eased the throttle forward and made for the spring, hoping they were still there, yet afraid they weren't. "What have I done?" he sobbed as he powered onto the bank below the spring. The eternity he had spent since he had left the spring had only been a few minutes in real time, but it was long enough for Charlie to pack up and leave, taking Betty with him. Orin was alone in the dark with his guilt. He reached in his cooler and popped the cap on another beer. He had to think. *What should I do?* Somewhere between beers he started thinking it wasn't his fault. The kid shouldn't have been right there in the middle of the river. It was almost dark too. I would've made the turn if the sight of the kid in the boat hadn't scared me into cutting it too hard. *What should I do?*

He made his decision and turned to leave, then remembered the watch. He took the watch from his pocket, looked at it as if it were something alive, then drew back and threw it to the center of the spring. *They won't find it there.* As the weight of the watch left his hand, he had no idea how heavy the memory of that watch in his hand would get.

He started his journey home that evening, with the throttle barely above idle. He gave his powerful motor just enough power to maintain control. The need for speed had left him along with his anger at Betty. He would not speak to another soul of the events of that evening, of the accident below the spring. *It was an accident,* he assured himself. An unbearable fear overcame him as he neared that spot on his way down river, a fear of discovery, blame and punishment. That fear crept through his alcohol soaked brain and just as strong came a sorrow, a sorrow that this had to happen to him more than a sorrow for the youth. No, he couldn't tell a soul, not even Betty.

He passed the tree which bore no signs of the tragic event which had occurred less than half an hour ago. His clouded mind cleared immediately as he caught the reflection of a bright object below the bend; it was the boy, lying face up in the shallows. "Could he still be alive?" he wondered. He nudged the boat into the sand next to the motionless form. He played his light on the youth, who lay face up, in utter stillness, with a strange, calm expression on his face, his mouth and eyes open. The light reflected off the water which filled his mouth, and he knew . . . there was no life here.

The boy had somehow freed himself from the clutches of the boat that had dragged him under; his life jacket now held his lifeless head above the water. He thought maybe he was dreaming this nightmare and would wake up the next morning and Betty would assure him that they had had an uneventful trip back from the spring. How wrong could he be?

What am I doin'? Orin asked himself under his breath as he lifted the youth's body from the shallows and laid it onto his deck. *What am I doin'?* The dull throb of his idling motor seemed to enter his brain and expand, searching for a way out. *Why don't I just leave him here?* His thoughts of carrying the boy out were being scrambled by the beer and the noise of his motor. He had lost his earmuffs somewhere along the way and couldn't find Betty's. "They're probably in her purse." He mumbled, as he droned on down the river, *he was dead, there is no connection to me, I could just say I found him lying there and had no idea what happened. It was an accident. They surely wouldn't hold me responsible for the boy's death if I reported it, would they? I could sober up before they got there. Where would I take him? To the sheriff's office? To the hospital? Should I just take him home and call them? Call who? Would they arrest me? Would they believe me if I told them I just found him? Would they put two and two together? They would surely wonder what sunk his boat?* His thoughts were reaching a higher revolution than the eight cylinders propelling him down river.

"God, I wish I had just left him there for the gators and hightailed it home," he shouted out loud, then immediately felt the weight of paranoia press him further into his seat. He knew no one lived on this stretch of river and he could only be heard by some late night fisherman and chances of that were slim. But this was the beginning stages of a paranoia which would eat at him the rest of his life, turning the words of others into suspicion where none existed, causing him to avoid situations and places which would expose him to the past, this past he was now creating.

The closer he got to his home, the more his anguish grew. He thought about Betty. *How would I explain it to her? Why hadn't I just left the body there in the shallows? The gators would have surely found it and gotten the blame for the whole thing. Then I wouldn't have to tell anyone. Who would know? Betty wouldn't understand, she would call me stupid and maybe even walk out as she had a couple of times before, leaving me to sort out my own problems. Maybe she would feel sorry for me, if I convinced her it was not my fault? After all it wasn't, that stupid kid just as well killed himself by stopping there in the middle of the river. I had tried to help him hadn't I? If that watch hadn't slipped off I might have been able to pull him up. The watch! Why didn't I keep it instead of flinging in the spring? It may have caused scratch marks on the boy's left wrist when it had slipped off in my grip. If I'd kept it, it would have proved to her that I had tried to help the boy.* "She has to help me get through this," he mumbled out loud.

He stopped at his home on the river long enough to figure out from the open drawers and missing Chevy that Betty wouldn't be helping him figure out anything tonight. She'd left him for sure this time. She'd never taken her clothes before and he'd always been able to talk her into staying when she came back to get them. His depression from this discovery nearly let him forget that he had a dead child in his boat and that he desperately needed to inform the authorities. He finally started to reach for the phone and stopped. *What if they don't believe me? What if they ask me why I couldn't pull him up? What if they find the watch? Should I tell them about the watch? What about the scratches on his arm if I don't tell them?* His mind whirled with these and other thoughts. These thoughts led him to another decision. The third bad decision which would be forever on his mind.

He stopped at the tool shed, picked up a shovel, hung Jimmy's life jacket in the rafters of his boat house, started *Wet Dream*, then continued down river to a spot he knew which was far enough from everything and everyone to hide the results of this night's work. He buried Jimmy that night with no headstone, no marker, no prayers to God, very little remorse, a subdued fear of discovery and an excessive amount of self pity. He sat in his living room later that night, drinking one beer after another until his consciousness left him. He slept the sleep of drunken stupor. Drunken stupor was to become the only sleep in his remaining days without the nightmare.

Yes, he felt the need for speed this night as well, but he knew that he would get over this night and find another Kathy to take Betty's place. Flying on the river like this left no time for dreams of women; this was when he was the happiest.

He had plenty of money now, not like before when he and Betty were married. Before, he could never seem to make ends meet. Betty had saved him from bankruptcy but he would never admit that to his conscious mind. After she left that awful night he nearly lost everything as he slipped into a conscious coma with his drinking and feeling sorry for himself. The scam he cooked up with Bobby had given him a new challenge and had pulled him out of the financial doldrums.

All this was behind him now and the new challenge was to get that bitch Kathy to move in with him or get a new girlfriend, whichever came first. He opened his mind to the rush of cool wind and concentrated on the river with its hidden rocks and overhanging trees. A strong light blinded him as he rounded a bend. It was flashing frantically as he throttled back. *That dumb son of a bitch is trying to get killed. Don't he know I can't see a thing with that God-damned light in my eyes?*

Chapter Thirty

It's working

Mike heard the high pitched whine of the airboat in the distance and put away the fishing rod. *Time to get ready.* If by some chance it wasn't Orin he would have to alter his plan. Not too many airboats ran the river at night, especially in this low water. Rocks right under the surface were a serious hazard, even to them with their shallow draft. He got his search light ready, took the cover off the engine and just waited. He had already coiled the two lines on the foredeck, one with a small snap shackle at the bitter end and another one aft. It sounded as if Orin was in good form; he was really revving *Wet Dream* up. *Damn,* he thought, *I hope he can stop in time after he sees me.*

The whine was fast becoming a throaty roar as the airboat drew closer. Then suddenly there he was running without lights. The rapids posed no threat for the airboats if the driver knew the river well, the airboats had no prop nor lower unit hanging deep in the water. The airboats skimmed across the water at barely six inches of depth when they were on a plane. When off plane, they only drew about one foot of water. In the daylight you could usually see rocks that close to the surface But at night you either had to be real good to go that fast or be real lucky. Mike had the idea that Orin was neither, just stupid. Mike had turned his search light on just as Orin rounded the last bend and flashed it wildly to get his attention and at last he heard him cut the throttle and watched him glide to a stop barely ten feet away. Mike clicked the light off.

"What the hell are you doin'?" Orin was screaming, "What the hell's goin' on? You dumb son of a bitch, you're anchored right in the middle of the channel." He had idled the engine down and was holding it against the current as best he could, yelling obscenities and shaking his fist.

"Hold on . . . Hold on." Mike was yelling back and waving the light. But he could see Orin still had his earmuffs on. He pointed to his own ears. Orin finally got the message and removed the earmuffs. "I need your help Mike yelled. Here, catch this line." He picked up the line he had coiled at the stern and gestured as if he were going to throw it."

Orin left the driver's seat and made his way forward to catch the line. He had calmed down some but was still mumbling to himself as he caught the line and made it fast. "What the hell's going on?" he said as they came close enough to communicate over the rumble of the engine. "I could have run right into you anchored in the middle of the channel like that. Specially with that fuckin' light in my eyes."

"I know said Mike," trying to sound sheepish, "I wasn't thinking too clear. I'm really upset with this damned boat. It just quit running and I have been trying to start it for half an hour. Now the battery's dead."

He studied Mike's face for a minute and said, "Hey, I know you. You're the guy I played pool against last week. What's your name? Mike ain't it, Mike, Tracy?"

"Yeah, that's right. Can you tow me to the boat ramp right up the river?"

"I don't like towin' people, it's dangerous, and beside that boat ramp is not right upriver, it's two miles upriver."

Mike knew where the boat ramp was and it was just the right distance for his needs. "I'll be glad to pay you," Mike pleaded, "I'll give you twenty bucks said Mike."

"Why don't you just tie your boat off to a cypress and I'll give you a ride to the ramp? I don't like to tow!" Orin exclaimed. "And besides that, my prop wash will blow you right off that boat."

"I don't want to leave it here, and I don't want to have to figure out how to come back and get it in the morning. I have to get it fixed first thing. I run a charter business and I've got a good paying run before noon," Mike pleaded. "OK, I'll give you fifty to tow me and help me get it on the trailer; I got a long line ready at the bow."

"Alright, alright, but I don't like it too much. Give me the fifty up front," he stated flatly.

Mike thought a minute, retrieved a fifty out of his wallet thinking to himself, *this will be worth the fifty,* handed it to Orin and said, "I've done this before. It'll be OK. Cut your engine and we'll walk your boat alongside mine. I'll fix the lines to your stern. Then you can start your engine and take up slack while I pull up my anchor."

Orin reached back and cut the engine. An ominous stillness fell over them like a blanket. They both paused for a second or two as the quietness gripped them. The normal night sounds had ceased in deference to the shouting and engine noise. Both men were acutely familiar with the natural sounds of the night creatures of the Withlacoochee, the endless chirping of the tree frogs, the chatter of busy raccoons, the screeching of owls and the throaty drum of the alligator. As eerie as these sounds were, the silence was worse.

Mike brought them back to reality as he untied the line off the stern and started to lead the airboat around the starboard side. Orin fended off and held onto the pontoon boat's rail. Mike asked him to hold the boats together as he secured the lines aft. Mike led the line he had previously coiled on his foredeck outside the rails and to the stern cleats of the airboat. He looped the line from one cleat to the other forming a bridle with the line doubling back to the bow of the pontoon boat. Out of Orin's view, Mike reached under the fuel tank on the airboat, found the clip on the end of the line he had left there earlier and clipped it onto a small loop he had fastened to the tow line. Mike then went forward and held the boats while Orin started the engine. When it was running smoothly, Mike motioned Orin to ease forward. As the airboat slowly pulled away, Mike started pulling in the anchor on the pontoon boat. Just as the towline came taut the anchor broke loose. *Everything's going too smoothly,* Mike thought.

The airboat's motor rumbled and the two boats started their slow dance upriver, the airboat leading and the pontoon boat following. Out of the narrows, around a short bend the river widened out. Mike reached for the tow bridle and unfastened the line from the starboard cleat and let it slip through his fingers. He felt, through the towline, the two barely detectable pulls and releases and said, It's working.

"Adios asshole," Mike whispered to himself.

Chapter Thirty-one

How did this happen?

Orin felt the forward surge as the towline started slipping from around the cleats of the air boat and if his motor hadn't been so loud he may have heard the metallic clink as the drain plug fell into the bilge and rattled overboard, or he may have heard the dry sucking as the fuel pump heaved for gas that wasn't there. But he didn't hear those things and the airboat soon began to sputter then died completely. His own cursing, and the earmuffs he wore for protection kept him from hearing the rush of water through the drain plug until the gurgle was swallowed by the surrounding water. When he finally realized that something was wrong, it was too late. He jumped from the pilot's seat down into the boat and felt the water around his ankles. With a slow awareness the fear set in. His boat was sinking. *What had happened?* The pontoon boat was drifting away, and Mike was standing at the bow motionless with his hands on his hips and a wide grin on his face. Orin's last-second-search turned up a life jacket which he clung to in desperation. The airboat lifted its bow as if in prayer and rushed to the bottom. Orin jumped aside so as not to be dragged down with it. It was not deep here and the airboat bumped to a stop as the stern hit bottom leaving about a foot of the prop cage above water. Orin reached for the artificial island and hung on for dear life. In the middle of the Withlacoochee, in the middle of the night, in the middle of nowhere. *How did this happen?* He had no idea this was all a careful plan, but he would soon learn.

Chapter Thirty-two

It soothes the soul

When Mike released the towline and pulled it back onto the deck of the pontoon boat, the small line with the clip attached to it pulled the loosened gas line from the fuel pump and the drain plug from the transom, then the line brought the plug right into Mike's hand where he held it and smiled. In one short pull he had disabled and sunk Orin's boat. He stood at the bow and savored the moment before heading aft to start his engine.

He shined his light on the sinking airboat and throttled slowly towards it. He could see Orin fumbling to put a life vest on while clinging to the prop cage inches above the water.

Mike eased up to within ten feet of Orin clinging to his little island and hovered there with just enough throttle to hold him against the lazy current. He threw the drain plug upstream just far enough to allow it to sink into the airboat on its' way to the bottom. He then went forward, lowered the anchor and let out line until he and Orin were about twenty-five feet apart. Then he waited for Orin to speak. The fun was about to begin.

"Hey, I thought your motor wouldn't run," Orin shouted.

"I lied," Mike replied.

Orin said, "What?"

Mike motioned towards the earmuffs. Orin got the message, angrily ripped off his earmuffs and threw them into the water. "What'd you say?"

"I said, I lied," Mike repeated.

"Why?" quizzed Orin with a hurt expression on his face.

"Swim over here and we can discuss it in comfort. I've got some dry things for you and I'll take you home. By the way, you need to hurry, I saw a big gator on the left bank just two days ago."

Orin still hadn't gotten the full picture, but he knew that the gator Mike was talking about was big because he had seen him just this afternoon in this same area. The pontoon boat was a hell of a lot safer than the remains of his airboat. He started swimming.

Mike waited for him at the front ladder. When Orin reached it and started to climb aboard Mike put his hand on Orin's head and shoved him backwards into the water. While Orin sputtered to the surface Mike released more anchor line to widen the distance between them.

Orin coughed and yelled, "What the hell's going on?"

"Come here and I'll tell you," Mike said grimly.

"What the fuck are you doin'?" Orin coughed.

"Oh, just trying to get something from you."

"What the hell d'you want from me? I guess you want your fifty back?" Orin sneered.

"Swim over here and I'll let you hang on the ladder while we discuss it."

Orin reviewed his options and said, "Let me come aboard you bastard. I'm getting cold and there's gators in here at night. What the hell did I ever do to you?"

"Oh, you didn't do anything to me. You did it to my friend and neighbor, little Jimmy Thompson."

Orin's heart stopped beating and the fear of gators and hypothermia took a back seat to the fear of discovery. The nightmare he had hidden all these years was coming again but this time it was coming while he was awake. *Maybe I passed out*, his hopeful mind wondered. *Maybe I'll wake up soon.*

Asleep or awake he knew he needed to get out of this river soon. "Hey, this is getting' serious. Let me out of here."

"I said you could come over and hang on."

"I want in the damn boat!" Orin said with a feeble effort of forcefulness.

"Suit yourself," said Mike, and made a move to haul up the anchor.

"What're you doing? You cain't leave me here?"

"Watch me asshole."

"Wait . . . wait, I'll come over."

Just as Orin was reaching for the ladder Mike quickly shoved his head under again.

Orin came up sputtering and gasping for breath. He had swallowed some water that time for sure. Mike reached out and grabbed him by the hair of his head and said, "Look asshole, we can make this easy or we can make it hard. The sooner you tell me what happened that night five years ago the sooner you get in this boat. I know damn well you killed him and you're going to tell me all about it starting with leaving the spring. You can consider this just a rehearsal—Buck Stone knows too."

"I didn't kill him, it was an accident, I swear," the first sign of humbleness creeping into his tone, as Orin realized that his five-year-old-secret had just been broadcast.

"Let me up and I'll tell you everything," he pleaded.

"I'll let you aboard when you finish and it all adds up."

Orin clung to the ladder keeping his legs as still as possible. He knew that gators could feel the vibrations of swimming animals and that all the thrashing would attract one sooner or later. He pleaded with Mike several times as he finally realized the hopelessness of holding back and he started to tell the story. His lasting sorrow for his own misfortune, not the boy's, brought tears to his eyes as he retold the incident. He embellished his part in trying to save the boy as much as he thought he could, with Mike dunking him a time or two when he thought he was getting less than the truth.

In fact Orin was feeling some relief by telling someone. He had longed to tell Betty that night when he first came home with the kid's body in the airboat. He had longed for her wisdom and advice. He blamed her absence instead of his weak character and drunken state of confusion for the bad decision to bury the body. Orin's fear of punishment and humiliation had caused him to imagine over the years just what that punishment might be. After all it had been an accident. He had acted as quickly and hard as he could to save the kid. Sure he had made a few mistakes: he should have reported it right away, he should not have thrown the boy's watch in the spring, he shouldn't have fished the boy out of the river, and he shouldn't have buried him. But what could they do to him for that? He really didn't have any idea but he had minimized it in his mind to the point where he sometimes contemplated telling the sheriff, at least the first part.

He couldn't help it if the boy was never found. They would have no way of knowing that he had buried the boy or of finding him even if they suspected.

    Mike listened to Orin with the old sadness shrouding him like a heavy coat. He wanted to shove this guy under and hold him there until the life left him. When Orin told of throwing the watch in and leaving the spring the second time, Mike started to see where this would end. He knew this guy's character. Mike's mind was working overtime. He questioned Orin about his trip downriver after the boy's death and Orin told him he passed the sunken boat and continued down river. Mike shoved him under violently, pulled his head above water and shoved him under again as he opened his mouth. "I hope you don't drown before I get what I came here for. You *do* know where he is, and you *are* going to tell me."
    He turned the sputtering head which he held by the hair and looked Orin in the eye. "Where is he?" he asked with those penetrating eyes boring into Orin's soul. Orin sobbed and shivered violently now. Mike knew it was about over. He repeated, "Where is he? And if you say, 'I don't know', so help me I'll drown you now and leave you for gator bait."
    Orin coughed and spit up water, struggling to keep his head above water against the downward effort of Mike's hand, his muddled, water soaked brain looking for a way out. He gathered his energy in a lunge for Mike's arm in an attempt to pull him into the water with him. He managed to get both hands on Mike's arm but had no leverage or weight to complete the effort. Mike's other hand was firmly attached to the Pontoon boat railing. He merely extended his reach to shove Orin further under. Orin's shortness of breath caused him to release Mike's arm and fight for the surface. He managed to grasp the bottom of the ladder and raise his head just above the surface as his lungs sucked in air and water. He shook and coughed throwing up water and suddenly went limp.
    Mike was afraid he had pushed him too far when Orin's lips started to move with no sound at all. He let him rest and breath for a short time without relaxing his grip on his hair. Orin

soon opened his eyes and stared at Mike with the same vacant look that Jimmy had witnessed five years ago. He had no fight left. He started sobbing.

Orin sobbed, "Oh, God, I'm sorry. I found him floating in the river after I left the spring. He was dead. I pulled him into the boat." He coughed some more and saw no mercy in Mike's dark stare. "I didn't know what to do, I was afraid they would think I killed him. I'm sorry, I didn't know what to do."

Mike looked at the pitiful excuse for a human and said, in a quiet voice, "I am asking one more time. Where is he?" And put a slight downward pressure on Orin's head. Those steely eyes continued to bore into Orin and he said, "You'll tell me the rest of the story now."

Orin, his eyes wide with terror, told the rest of the story, again trying to make his actions sound reasonable. Mike listened with a sick feeling in his gut. When Orin told about digging the shallow grave near the cypress tree, the one with the eagles nest, it occurred to Mike to ask what had happened to Jimmy's life jacket.

Orin hesitated a little too long and said, "I don't know."

Mike said, "You stupid son of a bitch, don't you know when it's over?" and ducked him again, this time holding him under until Orin's fight to the surface became frantic. He tried to climb Mike's arm but Orin's weak condition was no match for Mike's strength and commanding position. "Tell me what you did with it asshole, it was never recovered, and I know you wouldn't have buried it with him. You're smart enough to know it could have floated him out of a shallow grave during high water."

He told Mike he had hung the jacket in his boathouse rafters and Mike knew he had enough. He knew Bobby's info about the scam would not be needed now, at least not till later when he roasted this son of a bitch. Without a word he released Orin and started to haul in the anchor. Orin started to climb the ladder and Mike shoved him out and away one last time. He brought up the anchor with Orin pleading with him to let him aboard. As Mike motored just out of Orin's reach he said, "I would advise you to swim to shore right away and walk home. You'll have a better chance with the water moccasins than that big gator. By the way, keep the fifty." And Mike backed away, turned the boat downstream and eased the throttle forward.

Chapter Thirty-three

The end of a long day

Mike negotiated the rapids flawlessly on his return to Angler's. He tried to block Orin's words from his mind. He couldn't afford to screw up and wreck his boat now and that chore demanded his full attention. The anger he held in check swelled to bursting when he passed the cypress with the eagle's nest. He nearly turned around to finish the job. Instead he gestured to the spot—a half wave and half salute—as he said, "I'll make him pay."

He slowed to an idle and turned off his running lights before he rounded the last bend above Anglers. He wanted to be sure there were no night fishermen around. He was prepared to find a quiet cove and wait them out. He couldn't afford to be seen here tonight, at least not by anyone who knew him. It was still early and he could wait as long as he had to. But he had a long drive ahead of him and not much time to sleep after he got there before starting back. He was scheduled to meet Kurt about eleven o'clock tomorrow morning. Things had gone according to plan. *Very well, indeed. Perhaps too well?* He was sure Murphy's Law would strike at any minute. *Hey, cut it out, he thought. I've seen good plans fail because someone got jumpy, and now is no time to get jumpy.*

As he approached the docks he saw lights bounce off the building. "Flashlights," he mumbled under his breath. He was too close to turn back up stream, he would have to run the motor above idle to make headway into the current, and they would surely hear him. His heart was pumping overtime as he watched the lights bounce around. There were at least two lights and he heard voices that sounded high pitched, like they were excited about something, but they were still too far away for him to understand what they were saying. He had miscalculated in the dark and passed the point of no return before he saw the lights. He had no choice.

His space at the end of the docks had a little room upstream with a small eddy behind a large rock. He shifted into reverse as he nosed her gently into the eddy and let it hold his bow upstream. He turned to starboard to slow the stern which was still in the current. At the last second he shifted to forward and then cut the engine. He walked forward and fended off as the boat came to rest. *Perfect.* He held his breath as he listened. The voices were still talking excitedly only this time he could understand some of the conversation.

"Biggest God damned cat fish I ever seen," said number one who talked in a somewhat excited but more or less normal voice.

"Yeah," said number two in a high squeaky voice, "I'll bet he weighs thirty pounds."

Mike couldn't see them but figured from their tone that they were not yet aware of him. He crouched down below his rails and tied off the boat. He lay down on the portside and waited while the intrepid fishermen argued about what to do with this huge catfish. Number one, who apparently caught it, wanted to find a scale and weigh it. Number two wanted to take it home and show everybody. "We can put it in a wash tub until morning then take it down to the store and weigh it."

"Hell, if we take it home we can weigh it on the bathroom scales."

"Yeah, and we can take some pictures."

It didn't take long for Mike to figure out that these guys had a cooler of beer and were in no hurry to come to any conclusions as long as it lasted. One scheme after another, like waking up one of their buddies named Earl, and getting him involved, to calling a reporter that one of them knew to get his name in the paper. Mike knew he would have to come up with an alternate plan, or spend the rest of the night here on the dock.

He somehow got his boat cover in place without any undue noise, and they were still telling each other how big that catfish was. Mike couldn't place the voices but if they kept their boat here chances are they would know him even if he didn't know them. He could not just walk out of here the way he walked

122

in. The boat ramp was down past the docks and on the other side of the bridge. There was only one way to get past these clowns.

He undressed, put his clothes and a towel in his dry bag from the boat and slipped off the stern of the boat, this would be risky but he didn't have enough time to wait as long as these guys might take. Murphy had struck, now he had to pay the consequences. He didn't want to have to deal with his wet suit over at the launch ramp and in Kurt's car so he went in his birthday suit for the short swim under the bridge. This water was cold . . . He swam upstream with the help of the eddy, then angled across keeping the end of the docks between him and the flashing lights. When he was a good way upstream and on the far side of the river he started drifting with the current. He kept the dry bag between him and the docks and held it as deeply submerged as he could with enough above the surface to hide his head. He floated his way past the docks and under the bridge. The boat ramp and parking area had night lights and was well lit but deserted except for three cars, one of which was Kurt's rental. He swam in well below the ramp, and after watching in all directions and seeing no one, he rose and walked to the nearest cypress tree and stood in its shadow while he dried himself off and dressed.

He was shivering heavily in the cool night air and couldn't wait to get in the car for some heat, but caution was in order. Until he was driving away he could not be seen. The traffic was light and he had seen a police cruiser slide past towards town about five minutes ago, he waited for a break in the traffic and walked briskly through the launch area and parking lot to the car and got in. He started the engine, turned on the heater and lay down on the front seat soaking up the heat. He watched the road until he saw a lull in the already sparse traffic, then pulled out onto Highway 41 South.

His trip down the river had been too demanding to think much about the results of his meeting with Orin. His thoughts, other than driving the boat were filled with the nightmare of Orin's words. The images these words conjured up in his mind would help him complete his destruction of Orin Taylor. Driving back to Stuart gave him plenty of time to make plans toward that end.

He waited until he crossed I-75 to stop for coffee. The heater had done its job and eased the shivering and he was sure that no one at this truck stop would know him. Sometimes it didn't pay to be as well known as Mike. He wouldn't need to get out of the car again until he arrived in Stuart.

As he drove and sipped his coffee, he thought about Orin and what he had learned tonight. He wondered what Orin would do. Even if he kept his life jacket on for warmth he would get deeply chilled if he stayed in the water long enough to reach one of the houses downstream. That is if a gator didn't get him first. He really had seen a big one near that spot. Mike had chosen the spot as ideal to disable the airboat. It was the most inaccessible stretch of river. It was part of the Withlacoochee State Forest and most of it was swampy low land. If Orin didn't stay in the river he would have a hard time walking out. If he was smart he wouldn't do either. He would find him a piece of high ground or a big oak tree he could climb, make himself comfortable and wait out the night. The water moccasins were not that active this time of year. They were the least of Orin's worries. He could hail a fisherman the next day for a ride out. Mike doubted he was that smart. He mulled over Orin's account of what happened and tried to figure out how to finish this business. His first thought was, I'll turn the bastard in to Buck, and maybe I'll get the IRS involved. That should raise a shit storm. He thought that would be a good beginning. Then he realized he couldn't do that. What if the bastard dies tonight? Buck will want to know where I got the information. It would be hard enough to explain even if the bastard didn't die, and Mike thought he wouldn't die if he was halfway smart.

Mike didn't dwell on Orin's plight, whatever happened to him he deserved. If he was smart enough to get out of there alive Mike vowed to make Orin's life a hell on earth for what he did and he would start tomorrow.

Chapter Thirty-four

Survival

Orin was cold, but his shivering was from fright as much as the cold. Even dressed for the chill and with his life preserver helping to hold in his body heat, he knew he couldn't stay in this cold river all night and survive. Just the cold alone would get him if not the gators. He tried to think, but the emotional trauma he had just experienced was flooding his mind. His throat hurt and he felt sick from swallowing so much water; the bastard nearly drowned him. His first task was to get out of this river and get his bearings. How far was the nearest home downriver? Upriver? Could he walk out? Where was he? There wasn't enough of his cherished airboat showing to climb up on. He couldn't believe that the bastard had left him on this river in this condition.

He was smart enough to not thrash the water any more than he already had with that bastard dunking him. He thought the sound of their boats would have kept any gator away, up till now, but visions of the big gator he had seen earlier kept flashing in his mind. He had to get ashore. The only problem was there was not much shore in this stretch of the river. He knew vaguely where this episode left him, as his thoughts returned to his trip up the river from Kathy's (that bitch). He recalled the rapids he had negotiated and remembered passing the big dead cypress with the eagle's nest. He was in the middle of nowhere. That bastard knew exactly where on this river to pull this stunt.

He breast stroked quietly to the nearest bank or what seemed like a bank. It was mostly floating vegetation and he could touch bottom as he neared it but the bottom was mushy and wouldn't support his weight. As he sunk to his knees in the rotten mess, his life preserver floated up around his neck, he panicked

125

and grabbed for something to help pull him out of this muck. He reached out, his extended body keeping him from sinking in further. He was able to reach a hanging branch of cypress and pulled his legs free. The immediate problem of being stuck was solved, but one shoe remained two feet under the mud. That ended any thoughts of walking out.

Having learned a difficult lesson he continued crawling along in the shallow water, keeping his body extended, not trying to stand. He swam/crawled along in this fashion searching for solid ground. The terrifying threat of water moccasins was foremost on his mind as he searched for someplace to pull himself out. He knew the moccasins were well populated along the river and that they could be very aggressive. He'd heard stories of them dropping into boats, chasing swimmers and such. He also knew that if bitten he would never get to a hospital in time for the anti-venom to be effective, if he could make it there at all. This fear seemed well grounded as he worked his way along the shoreline. Each floating branch became a snake and half submerged trees became gators. He was exhausted and shivering relentlessly when he finally found some footing several yards away from the main river and raised himself out of the water. He knelt on hands and knees as he worked his way to higher ground. Several feet inshore the ground got firmer and he crawled with increased vigor as he realized he had finally managed to get well above the river. The ground there lay mounded up with leaves and small twigs. It felt spongy and good as he lay prone in his exhaustion, curled into the fetal position, too weak and cold to think as he drifted into a stupor just short of sleep.

Chapter Thirty-five

Predator

The yellow eyes narrowed, piercing the darkness, the vertical slits of his pupils focused on a movement. Something moved, entering his world. He lay unseen amongst the floating vegetation, only his eyes and nose above the dark water. His clear, secondary eyelids closed, allowing him to keep his eyes open, as he silently submerged. He picked up vibrations of something at the water's edge. His smooth undulations brought him closer as he controlled his depth just above the murky bottom.

His eating habits were strange, he would gorge himself in spurts then lay about for days digesting the meal. His system would only allow the digestion process when his cold blooded central system reached 60 or 70 degrees. He had to absorb a lot of sunlight in the daytime to keep his body temperature up; the ridges and bumps on his back were filled with a fatty substance which stored the heat from sunlight. He had been in hibernation through most of the winter, dug into the mud, surviving on the stored energy from the fall. He moved slowly, fully awake now, and hungry.

His presence dominated the river. He stalked at night, homing in on sounds and vibrations with excellent night vision to guide him to his prey, a killing machine designed over hundreds of thousands of years, shaped to perfection by trial and error. He feared nothing including man, but would shy away from the presence of man, seemingly not from fear as much as from annoyance and then only in the daylight hours. He moved fast and stealthy in the water, able to swim up to 18 miles per hour, and he could lay for hours at the edge of a bank without movement waiting for some animal to come for a drink. He could run on land nearly as fast as a man for short distances. At 14 feet in length and a hefty 1,200 pounds, he was a formidable beast of prey. He and many others like him ruled the nights on the Withlacoochee River.

He could now see the shape silhouetted against the night sky as the large water moccasin entered the water. With incredible speed his open mouth broke the surface and his jaws seized the unfortunate snake with a tremendous closing force. There could be no escape. The struggle, a violent, twisting roll designed to tear limbs or huge chunks off larger victims, was his way of reducing his meal to swallowing size. His inability to chew his food dictated this method of eating and it proved very effective with larger animals. It was completely wasted on his five pound prey. The gator gobbled the snake down whole while still squirming, a small tidbit in his substantial diet. He would search for more.

The gator hunted unsuccessfully until the pre-dawn light silhouetted the lacey branches of the cypress trees. The huge gator ambled from the water to his favorite basking spot, a soft pile of rotting vegetation, the remains of some female's nest from a previous time. Built above the surrounding swampy ground, it offered a dry soft bed and cleared area, which allowed sunlight to penetrate the dense undergrowth, perfect for basking in the sun and secluded enough to keep his snoozes uninterrupted.

Chapter Thirty-six

Still out of town

Mike was back in the motel room at Stuart and sound asleep before dawn. As exhausted as he was, his sleep was tormented with heavy dreams which kept him tossing and turning, in silent combat with the covers and then the pillow. He seldom remembered his dreams and when he was able to recapture them it was usually through considerable effort. He could wake from a heavy dream and know he had been dreaming, his mind struggling to get a handle on the dream, and sometimes he would recall, but not this time.

He awoke to the obscene, incessant ring of his prearranged wakeup call. It took him a few minutes to realize just where he was and answer the call. A few minutes later the impact of all that had happened in the last twenty-four hours sent his brain wheeling. He tried to remember the details of a plan he had worked out during the drive here last night, but his brain was still fuzzy. He needed coffee, as if the two gallons he consumed last night wasn't enough. He really needed food. He had to meet Kurt in half an hour at the Pancake house across the street. A good cold shower would get him started. He wanted to be sharp when he talked to Kurt.

The shower felt good and he felt better as he crossed the parking lot and street towards the restaurant. He noticed his pickup in the lot. God, he was hungry. He hadn't eaten a substantial meal since lunch the day before. He entered, saw Kurt at a window booth and joined him. It had been a few years since they had had a decent conversation and aside from their brief meeting yesterday it had been that long since they had seen each other. Their bond remained such that they didn't need small talk, it was as if they had been meeting and talking on a regular basis. They knew the important subject and got right to it.

"How'd it go, buddy? You look like shit." Said Kurt.

"Thanks, I needed that," Mike said with a sheepish grin and then replied, "It went well thank you. I don't think there were any hitches, at least there were none that I knew about. I had a little trouble near the end but a nice cold swim solved that problem."

Mike ordered two eggs over medium with sausage and three pancakes on the side. His mind was clearer now, and he ordered de-cafe coffee to start ridding his system of his caffeine overload.

"Was it like you suspected?" Kurt asked.

"Pretty much. I knew this asshole was involved someway. I just didn't how much he was involved and how much of an asshole he was. You wouldn't believe what he did. It wasn't his stupidity as much as his selfishness that got him in so deep. The only thing he did right was cover it all up by just keeping his mouth shut. There was no one else involved and he kept it that way. From the way he babbled when he finally started telling me the truth, I think he was glad to get it off his chest. His relief is going to be short lived if I have anything to say about it." Mike then related Orin's story, at least Orin's version, which surprisingly held very close to the truth.

Kurt listened, without interruption, to Mike's version of the events of that night as told to him by Orin, his mouth agape. Mike finished his breakfast and Orin's version of the true story about the same time. Kurt just looked at him for several seconds, then said, "Where is this poor excuse for humanity now? And what are you going to do with him?"

"He is probably back home by now if he is smart and resourceful or he could be dead if he isn't smart. Either way his airboat is providing cover for the bass in the Withlacoochee and more importantly, I am about to disclose the whole episode."

"I suppose you have figured out how to do that without implicating yourself in this guy's misfortune?"

"You bet I have. And one way or the other this guy's going to pay." Mike disclosed his plan to Kurt, they caught up on some personal gossip and Mike was on his way shortly after noon, Mike in his pickup and Kurt in the rental. Mike would make a long phone call on his way home, and would still arrive at Stump-knockers in time for his prearranged dinner with the Banners.

Chapter Thirty-seven

Sunk

Buck Stone received the call while he drove in to the office. A few minutes after seven, the modern miracle of cell phones made this early news possible. Two early morning fishermen had spotted the top of a sunken airboat with no one around and had called it in on a cell phone. "Jesus Christ," Buck said out loud, "what's goin' to happen next?" He pondered the implications of a sunken airboat with no one around. "Must of happened last night? He wondered why no one had reported it then. He told Josey, who had taken the call and relayed it, that he was on his way to the office. He wanted to get a cup of coffee and make a few calls to figure out what was going on. It was shift change time and he wanted to take care of this himself. He would have to report it to the Fish and Wildlife people who had some responsibility in operations on the river. They would have to get the boat out of the river. He would have to figure out if a more serious crime than abandoning a boat in the middle of the river had taken place. Four Minutes later he pulled into his parking spot as Tommy pulled out of his.

He got out and walked over to Tommy's window. "Mornin' Tom, were you here when this airboat call came in?"

Tommy nodded and said, "Yeah, I was here. Josey took the call and wrote everything down including the telephone number of the fisherman who reported it. I got a run to make on a fender bender over on SR 200, call me if you need me. Something about that airboat doesn't add up."

"OK," Buck said as Tommy pulled away. He rushed inside and went straight to Josey, who monitored the radio until Barb came in at eight. "What've you got on that airboat Josey?"

as she tore a sheet off her pad without a word and handed it to him. He read the notes and went directly to his office, picked up the phone and dialed the fisherman's number.

"Yeah," a heavy voice said, "this is Buddy Ray."

"Buddy, this is Deputy Sheriff Stone."

"Yeah, sheriff, what can I do for you?"

"You can start by tellin' me where you are."

"Hell, sheriff, I'm still right here on the river."

"Just exactly where on the river, Buddy? Are you still at the sunken boat?

"Naw, we left as soon as we reported it. We're about a mile down river from there and still picking up stuff floatin' out that damn boat. We got life preservers and plastic oil bottles, a couple of cushions, a pair of earmuffs, a wooden boat hook and plenty of beer cans, some of 'em still full."

"Buddy," Buck interrupted, "I'm not too concerned with a detailed report of that boat's gear. What I am interested in is who it belongs to. Do you think you might do me a favor and run back upriver and try to identify that boat for me?"

"Why sure sheriff," Buddy stammered, "but what for?"

"You mean why identify the boat?" Buck couldn't believe this guy.

"No, sheriff. Why do you want me to run back up river?"

"You said it was partially out of the water, could you read the registration numbers on the rudders or read the name on the transom?"

"Reckon I could get them numbers for you, but I can tell you the name of the boat right now."

He said, "How's that, Buddy?" Buck tried not to show the frustration in his voice at how slow this conversation was going. He needed Buddy's help, it was the best he had.

"Well it's printed right here on these preservers," Buddy offered, then clammed up.

Buck sighed as he thought about the stupid people he had to deal with as he imagined Buddy Ray chuckling with his hand over the phone. Then he said in a voice, perhaps a little too condescending, "Would you like to tell me now, Buddy?"

"Sure, sheriff, its *Wet Dream*."

Buck's blood ran cold. *What the hell?* He recovered quickly and asked, "Did you see anyone around or any sign of foul play?"

"No," replied Buddy, "we didn't see nothin' but a sunken boat and lots of shit floatin' around."

"What mile marker is the boat nearest?"

"It's about a quarter mile upstream of marker 19, and it's right in the middle of the river."

"Buddy, this is important. I want you to search along the river as best you can. Gather up anything else you think might belongs to this boat and look for the owner who might have been stranded on the river all night. Call if you find anything important. We're on the way. And, Buddy," Buck said in his most official voice, "I really appreciate your help. Thanks . . . What's that? . . . Yeah, Yeah, you can keep the full beers."

He hung up and asked Josey to find Orin Taylor's number and call until she got him. If he wasn't home try his work. Oh, see if he has a girlfriend, he might be there. Buck was certain he had Orin on file. "And Josey, please stay on this even after Barb arrives. I'm heading for Angler's, tell Tommy to call me when he's free. But I want a report on the whereabouts of Orin ASAP." and he shot out the door.

Chapter Thirty-eight

Missing

Kathy Brannon knew she had to end it. It had taken her only one month, at one or two dates a week, to discover the true Orin. It was uncanny how strong and confident he could appear at times and how paranoid and insecure he actually was. She assumed his fits of anger, always accompanied by a blustery show of manliness, merely covered his frustration at being unable to control a given situation. She had seen this frustration and subsequent anger surface more often, with more intensity, and with less provocation in recent days.

He'd asked her to move in with him after only a couple of dates. She would decline and at first he would just sulk. As time passed he became more insistent with streaks of anger leading to last night's violent action. She had sensed the danger earlier and it frightened her. Last night was the final clue to her rude awakening. She had seen the same pattern in her father. It had eventually driven her away from her home at too early an age. Her mother had stayed to shoulder the burden of her father's misdirected anger, until his death by his own hand.

His violent nature caught up with him one rainy night, when his inability to control the situation led him to throwing a few items across the living room, then breaking down the bedroom door to give her mom a few new bruises and finally leaving in a huff to get more liquor. The roads were slick with rain and his lack of control took him off the road and down the Tennessee mountainside where a tree put an end to her mom's suffering. Her mom moved to Florida to be near her daughter and never looked back.

Last night brought back the memories she had long filed away in the farthest corners of her mind, after her mother's death a few years ago. All night long she heard the arguments that had awakened her so long ago as she lay listening, helpless to prevent the violence which always came. She recalled her mom's swollen face the next day and her father passed out on the couch, or bed, or wherever the liquor overtook him.

She woke up with these thoughts still tormenting her in her dreamlike state. The phone was ringing. She picked it up and said, "Hello," expecting it to be Orin in one of his apologetic moods.

"Hello, this is Josey Collins from the Citrus County Sheriff's Office and I'm checking on the whereabouts of Orin Taylor. Is he there?"

There was a collective moment of silence then Kathy answered with, "No. May I ask why you are asking?"

"I have no idea," Josey replied, which was not the whole truth. "Deputy Sheriff Stone asked me to find him and you are on my list to call."

"I haven't seen him since last night," Kathy replied rather shortly.

"What time did you last see him, miss?"

"About eleven o'clock. Excuse me, but what's this all about?"

"I really can't say, miss. Just one more question please. How did he leave?"

"What do you mean?"

"I'm sorry," Josey apologized, "I meant what kind of transportation did he use?"

Kathy chuckled as she said, "He left in his airboat and roared off up the river." Her amusement at Josey's question broke the tension and she continued, "I had a rough night," she explained, "and I thought you meant what kind of mood was he in when he left."

Josey, not one for idle conversation was interested in her answer and asked, "What kind of mood was he in?"

"Angry," Kathy answered, "and a little drunk." She saw an ally in Josey and she was eager to share her experience of last night. She went on, "We had an argument and he slapped me hard in the face then left angry, mumbling obscenities."

"Did you want to file charges against him?" Josey asked.

"No," she said in a subdued voice, "I don't think I'll see him again anyway."

Josey told her thanks and good bye and thought about it as she hung up. *You don't know how right you may be.*

Chapter Thirty-nine

The search

Buck had reached Angler's by the time Josey had found out that Orin wasn't home and that he didn't show up for work. It was the first time Orin had failed to show up at work in over a year. He sometimes remained under the influence, but nonetheless showed up. Josey had talked to his boss and found out that he normally didn't work on Saturday but they had some heavy duty maintenance scheduled and Orin needed to be there. His boss was hot.

Buck had called the Fish & Wildlife guys to meet him at Angler's and they were pulling in about the time Buck finished talking to the folks in the office. He knew Mike Tracy worked his fishing boat out of Angler's and he asked a few questions about when they had last seen Mike. He wasn't sure why he wanted to know; just that he had the feeling he should know. They hadn't seen Mike for two days, and no his boat hasn't moved.

Gerry Grant had launched the Fish & Wildlife runabout and pulled up to the Angler dock. Buck stepped in and said, "Mornin' Gerry, how's tricks?"

"Good Buck, except I would rather be fishin' than ridin' around with you."

"Likewise, Grumpy, I got lots of things better to do. But, duty calls," he replied as he smiled and clapped him on the back. Let's get to it. I'll fill you in on the way up river." He told Gerry about the sunken boat and asked him to make arrangements to have it raised as soon as possible and to treat it like a crime scene until a few questions got answered. He wanted to know why the boat had sunk. But most of all he wanted to find the owner. He didn't allude to any connection to the Jimmy Thompson affair, but in his heart he suspected there was. It seemed a strange coincidence that just as he started getting some evidence against Orin, in the disappearance of Jimmy Thompson, Orin's boat sinks under mysterious circumstances and Orin turns up missing. He did not believe in coincidence and would try to make the connection if there was one.

They found Buddy Ray and his friend still looking for flotsam. They transferred the items to Gerry's boat and thanked the fishermen for their efforts, then said they could quit looking. They asked them where they had searched and then sped on up river to the sunken boat. They pulled right up to it and tied off to the prop screen letting their boat hang downstream in the current which was not very strong in this part of the river. They could read the numbers clearly and called them in for a check, but Buck knew it was Orin's boat.

Buck still had Josey checking on Orin through anyone who knew him. She had found out he had a girlfriend and had located her at her home. The girl said Orin had left her place late last night and that he had headed up river. No, she didn't know what time but it was before midnight. Yes, he was by himself, had been drinking and was angry. Buck knew this put a different light on things whether there was a connection or not. At the very least he had a missing person and he didn't want to think about the worst case even though his gut was screaming it at him. He wanted this guy found.

He told Gerry what Josey had said and Gerry whistled. Then he said under his breath, "Wow, I wouldn't want to be on this river at night without a boat. Especially this time of year." Buck knowing full well he was referring to the gators and their habits during mating season. The males get real aggressive during mating season.

Buck said "We better start a serious search." and reached for his phone to call the Sheriff's Office in Inverness. He requested and got clearance for an immediate helicopter search. They would be here within minutes. In the meantime he and Gerry would search the banks. Buck said, "If it was me I would find a dry spot and wait out the night. The only dry spot might be up a tree if he could find one to climb."

"It looks like someone would have spotted him or he would have hollered them down," said Gerry as he untied the boat and started the motor, "He surely couldn't be that far from the river?"

"Yeah," said Buck, his mind elsewhere.

They did a slow search along the banks, looking for any sign that might indicate where he might have left the river. But the banks here were almost non existent, offering no indication that it wasn't just another day on the river. There were small creeks opening into small sloughs and water everywhere. It was frustrating searching. Buck recalled the search for Jimmy further up where the river was more defined, where the river gave way to solid banks three feet above the water in most places. This narrowed the search area. This was impossible, with the main river and the attending swampland extending the search area a mile or more in width.

The helicopter found from the air what they couldn't have seen from the water. They had to call Animal Control before they could approach the scene by boat, but from the air it could be seen in great detail. It was clear from 200 ft. up that a large gator had ended their search for a missing person. The gator was still there and they wanted him dead before he slid into the water and became just another big gator. It was Animal Control's policy to relocate small, problem gators near populated areas and to exterminate large, problem gators since relocation didn't work very well with older gators. Some had returned as much as fifty miles to reestablish and guard their territory. This was a large gator and he had tasted human blood. They waited while another chopper flew in a sharpshooter from Animal Control who promptly dispatched the gator with one well placed shot. They then moved in cautiously right behind the experts with rifles.

Orin had not died easily. The struggle had taken place just beyond the dry mound of leaves, dirt and rotten vegetation. It looked like quite a battle scene. A gator automatically clamps down on anything and immediately rolls tearing off chunks or appendages if the victim is too large to swallow whole. Gators can't chew but swallow large pieces to digest later. Orin's left arm was gone, torn off at the elbow and there were teeth marks around the head. Blood had splashed everywhere, showing that he had thrashed in a huge circle, his life gushing away. His life jacket had stayed on and the upper part was in shreds. It had apparently kept the gator from biting his head off. It looked apparent that Orin had died from loss of blood but they would do an autopsy on him to make sure, and on the gator to make sure they had the right one. The grisly scene produced silence among those present. They brought his body out into the boat and the Medivac chopper came and air lifted him to the hospital for the coroner to examine and pronounce dead. He would then be transferred to the morgue for the autopsy. The gator would suffer the same fate from different hands, then be skinned and his hide sold to help finance Animal Control.

———————

Gerry drove Buck back to Anglers and then went back to the boat. It would be a long day for him if he could even get done. He had called a local dock company in the area that had a small barge setting pilings for a new dock about four miles upriver. It would take him about an hour to get here. The powerful winch on the boat could lift the airboat free of the Withlacoochee. They may have to continue in the morning. If so, he would have to set out markers. Buck wished him luck and asked him to call him after the boat was up. He wanted to know what sank her.

Buck hightailed it back to the office after a brief conversation with a reporter from Channel 9 out of Tampa. He had a camera man with him and the red light was on. Marge would be coming in at four o'clock for the second shift and he wanted to brief her personally on this Orin business, plus have her fill out some paperwork. She was about the only one who could read his writing. He had scribbled some notes while he was riding back to Anglers and they were even worse than usual. He wanted a good report filed on this one. He wasn't sure it was over. She could get his report into the computer for him to edit later.

Chapter Forty

Death on the Withlacoochee

Robert Hastings was a good reporter. His specialty was crime reporting and he loved to put his own slant on it whenever possible. His editor gave him plenty of slack. As he hung up the phone he knew in his gut he had a great story here, one he could editorialize on and milk to the fullest. The caller had chosen him well. He had covered this same story five years ago and it was a real tear-jerker. He covered tragedy after tragedy and never got used to it; several stories stayed with him long after they were finished. This one stayed with him and never was finished. He lived in Citrus County, wrote for the biggest newspaper in central Florida, was an outdoorsman and stayed active in many of the area conservation projects. The story was right up his alley. It was a bombshell if it was true. He also knew he would have to hustle to check the facts offered and get a story in before tomorrow's deadline, the Sunday Times. He had to promise to do that and several other things before he was fed the first of the information. His information would come in stages starting with the crime and ending with evidence leading to the identity of the man responsible. The first information he was given, he knew to be true for he had a good memory.

Robert first checked out the background and found all that to be in order. At least this guy had his facts straight. He next roughed out his first article. It would be a shocker. Even if part of it was not true it would create a stir and he wouldn't be blamed. But he was seldom wrong about his gut feelings and this guy was very convincing. Robert was convinced that his informer knew everything there was to know about this five year old crime. He tried to convince the guy that his identity would not be disclosed if he confided in him. Robert told him it would increase his own confidence in the accuracy of the information, but the guy wouldn't relent. He finished the rough draft then made the phone call he had promised to make in order to gain permission to print the article. This had been part of the deal with his informant. Robert's article when finished looked like this and would be printed the following Morning.

DEATH ON THE WITHLACOOCHEE

This story began five years ago. It is a tale of the unbe-lievable behavior of a human being. We read the papers and watch television so we know the violent and unfeeling acts that we as humans are capable of. Some are unspeakable in their nature, the serial killers that prey on innocent victims, mad bombers with sick reasons to kill or maim their fellow citizens. These and other stories flood the media sometimes squeezing out the good in our lives. Do we get so callous that it takes something this horrible to get our attention? We, the press, are duty bound to report these things and we have a moral obligation to not glorify these senseless acts. It is in this light that this story is told. It is about the nature of human beings, both good and bad. It is about apathy, callousness, indifference, maybe evil and maybe murder.

This writer doesn't know the whole story, it is being told second hand and bit by bit. But I do know this; if it is true and I believe it is, you will wonder, as I do, what kind of human can be responsible for an act of this nature, an act not of insanity or purposeful hatred, but an act of senseless inhumanity. I have no names to give you. It is possible that the person telling this story is the person who did the deed; although he says he is not.

Jimmy Thompson was a fisherman, and although he was only fourteen-years-old at the time, he was a good fisherman. On the evening of March 25th, five years ago, he disappeared while fishing on the Withlacoochee River. His sunken boat was found the next day along with most of the gear in the boat. An extensive search by the authorities brought up nothing. It was viewed as a tragic accident as there was no sign of foul play. However, there was one enormous clue that nearly everyone overlooked or perhaps ignored. Was it overlooked because of our indifference? Have we become hardened to events seemingly more horrible than this? Are we too willing to accept these kinds of consequences at face value? Was this too small a tragedy to demand our attention?

There is no one person to blame for overlooking or ignoring this clue. What is it? It is the fact that Jimmy's body was never found. How can that be a clue? It is a clue because under natural circumstances, it would have been found. Sure there was talk of a gator dragging him into a swampy area but those in the know about gators know that they can't just eat an animal the size of a human. They can only tear off relatively small pieces and swallow them whole; they can't chew their food as we do. Under normal circumstances the body would have been found even in the remote areas near the accident, if it was an accident. At the time of year this happened the trees are mostly bare and visibility from the air is great. And there was a concentrated and immediate effort by police helicopters, an extensive search. There was good reason to believe that Jimmy was wearing a bright yellow life jacket with his name on the collar. It was not found either. In short there were two items, together or apart each highly visible which had disappeared without a trace. As they say in sports when second guessing a coach, "Hind sight is 20/20". I now know why, neither the body nor the life preserver was never found, because I have been told by someone who knows, and that knowledge precludes normal conditions.

There are at least two people who did not overlook or ignore this clue. James and Jenny Thompson were Jimmy's grand parents and guardians, and in their hearts and actions they still search for Jimmy's body. This is the essence of the crime. The fact that whatever or whoever took Jimmy from them didn't leave a body for them to bury. There was never any way to squelch this burning desire to find either Jimmy alive, or his body if he was indeed dead. No way to put an end to the nightmare. To grieve over a dead loved one, and put their soul to rest along with their body is one thing. To never know an end is another form of misery. I feel for Jim and Jenny, for the crime against them is real and unforgivable. I talked to them last night and received permission to print this story. The grief I encountered over the phone tore at my heart until it was nearly unbearable. In the end they will be relieved. It is with great sadness but some hope of

143

relief for the Thompsons that I offer the last paragraph and sentence in this story. It is directed to Deputy Sheriff Ballard (Buck) Stone in the hope that he will follow these directions to find and extract Jimmy Thompson's remains from the grasp of the Withlacoochee, where they have been buried in a hidden grave for five years. For obvious reasons I cannot disclose the site to anyone but the proper authorities.

Sheriff Stone, call the St. Petersburg Times and ask for me and I will give you detailed instructions where to look.

(To be continued Monday)

———————

Robert decided to withhold some of the information for the next day. He didn't want to stick his neck out too far and the proof of what he had written so far was under the cypress tree. The caller promised to call early the next day with additional details that promised to lead the sheriff to the identity of the responsible person. This much would start the wheels turning. He would have the rest of the story tomorrow afternoon when the sheriff located the body. He sent it to the editor's desk with a request for the front page, if they had room. He hadn't yet heard the news about a gator attack on the Withlacoochee River.

Chapter Forty-one

Gut feelings are hard to ignore

It was going on five o'clock when Buck finished briefing Marge and got her started on the report. He had asked Barb to work over, to handle the phone and radio traffic so Marge could concentrate. The three girls did a fantastic job at dispatch. They each took shorthand and could figure out which calls to put through to where or to whom. They knew the right questions to ask and could separate the emergencies from the not so urgent. It was a small office, just him, three deputies and the three girls on dispatch. He had a small office with a window overlooking the rest of the office. There was a small holding cell and the lavatories; the rest was just an open room with banisters separating the other desks. The deputies shared a desk and three sets of file cabinets. The Dispatchers shared a good sized work area with two computers, printers, fax, copier and various other office machines.

He now sat at his old oak desk, a scarred and battered looking relic. But somehow friendlier than one of those cold metal contraptions the county furnished. He had purchased this one with his own money at Howard's Flea Market over in Homosassa. He had drawn the shades on his window and closed the door. They didn't disturb him when he had his door closed unless it was real important. He leaned forward in his deep thought position. This position seemed to allow his thoughts to gather in front of him as if on a computer screen. And he could scroll through them selecting those which seemed relevant. This time the subject was Mike Tracy.

He wondered if Mike could be involved in this Orin business? *My guts say yes, he is. But how? I really want that initial report from Gerry Grant. And if that report shows nothing to indicate foul play to sink the boat, I'll look at the boat myself. Hell, I would do that anyway,* he thought. He guessed he wouldn't get that report until morning since it would soon be dark.

The fact that Orin had his life jacket on indicated that he was somewhat prepared. These airboat guys seldom wear their life jackets under normal circumstances. It was like he had plenty of time to grab it and put it on. There's nothing to indicate that this was anything but an accident. There's nothing to indicate that anyone, let alone Mike Tracy, was involved. According to the fellow at Anglers Mike hadn't even had his boat out for two days. There's no other way to get to that area of the river except by boat and how could Mike be involved without being there? He had a boat at Stump Knockers also, he could have come down from upriver. He needed to verify his whereabouts. *Damn, why am I so concerned about Mike Tracy?* Mike would take some sort of direct action if he thought the authorities weren't going to. But how could Mike even suspect Orin was as heavily involved as I know he was? He didn't have the information that I have. Or did he? Jim could have told him about the watch. He probably did. He could have found something about Orin from Charlie even though I asked Charlie to keep it quiet. How could he have known about Orin being alone on his way down river? I need to talk to Mike sometime today and maybe Charlie tomorrow.

His intercom button went off and brought him back to the real world. It was Marge; she reminded him that he wanted to watch the coverage of the incident on the six o'clock news. At least two news agencies had heard the reports of the incident and had dispatched their news choppers to buzz the area. Buck had been interviewed as soon as he stepped off the boat at Anglers. He had given them only the briefest of interviews and very few facts. They were treating it as an unfortunate boating accident and gator attack. They were withholding the victim's name pending notification of next of kin. He knew how relentless these people were. He wanted to see how much they had found out from other sources. He turned on the TV and poured himself a cup of the ever present coffee.

He watched and sipped his coffee as the handsome anchor man spoke the lead story and then turned it over to their man on the spot and showed Buck's interview on camera with the local news hound. They had some great overhead shots of the final grisly scene as they were removing the body with the dead alligator in the same frame. He knew there would be more at ten o'clock. There had been several phone calls requesting information or people wanting to talk to him. His dispatchers were doing a good job of holding them off. He checked with Marge who was watching the other TV tuned to the other main station. It was essentially the same.

Buck knew he had to stay on top of this. It would develop quickly. He turned off the TV and dialed the number for Mike Tracy's Scenic River Tours and got Mike's recorder. He asked Mike to call him and left his number. Then he dialed the number for Stumpknockers, thinking to leave a message, and asked for Mike Tracy. They said, "Hold on." After a long wait Mike came on the line, "Cap'n Mike."

"Hey Mike, this is Sheriff Stone. I need to talk to you."

"Go ahead but make it short. I got dinner coming."

"No, I mean I need to talk to you in person. Can I come over tonight?"

"Sure," Mike said, "I'm going to be late getting away from here though. I'm eating with the Banners tonight."

"You name the time and place and I'll be there."

Mike had expected to hear from Buck but not until he read the papers in the morning. "If it can't wait, I should be through here about eight o'clock and home fifteen minutes later."

"I'll see you then," said Buck.

Mike returned to the table with the Banners. "Sorry about that," said Mike.

"No problem," Al replied and Sarah seconded.

There was a short silence with Al and Sarah waiting for Mike to explain. Al soon saw that he wasn't going to, and so changed the subject. "You were telling us about your friend Kurt."

"Oh Yeah," Mike replied, and continued, "Kurt and I were diving on this sunken cruiser off Big Pine Key. Kurt was lead diver and we found her at depth of 150 feet still sitting upright. This was before the new nitrox mixtures and we only had a few minutes of bottom time on regular air. Kurt decided to enter and look for the owners wallet. It was rumored that he left in such a hurry he left it laying on the nav station with near a thousand dollars in it. We were young then, still crazy and a thousand dollars was big money to us. We both had our dive lights on. The visibility was poor from turbulence of current and it was dark at that depth in the cabin. We entered and it was like nothing you have ever seen. All of the wooden furniture was on the ceiling trying to get to the surface including the refrigerator. It was like a jungle and to make matters worse my dive light decided to crap out. Visibility was so bad that when Kurt would turn away from me all I could see was an eerie glow. I was scared shitless and Kurt was going on down into that mess like it was a swim in the pool. I knew if he left me there with no light I would never find my way out in time, so I lunged forward grabbed his fin, crawled up his leg and locked my hand onto his weight belt. He wasn't getting out of here without me. He struggled frantically to turn and tried to shove me away not realizing my situation. When he finally managed to turn his upper body towards me and the beam from his light showed me his face I broke out laughing. I saw the terror in his eyes and knew how bad I had scared him grabbing him that way. He saw me laughing with bubbles coming out the side of my mask and started laughing too. We almost forgot where we were."

"We recovered, swam out of there, and started our assent still chuckling. I guess the wallet with the thousand in it is still down there somewhere. That was one of our first dives together and we still get a kick out reliving those crazy times. We learned to trust each other beyond doubt. We each knew the other would give his life if the situation called for it." Mike finished his narrative with thoughts of his recent visit with Kurt, knowing full well Kurt would keep his end of the bargain.

After dinner Mike said his farewells, excused himself and went to meet Buck Stone.

Chapter Forty-two

The Alibi

Buck was waiting in the drive when Mike pulled in. He must really be in a hurry, Mike thought. *Damn, there's no way he could know anything about last night.* Unless Orin told him and I doubt that. And if he did I can still deny it. They would have a tough time proving it.

"Hey, Buck, how's it going?" Mike said as he walked toward the cruiser where Buck was leaning against the fender. "You must be in a hurry to see me." Mike decided to be direct.

"Not so much in a hurry as just anxious," Buck replied. "I have a lot going on and this is high on my list."

"Well," said Mike, "let's go in on the porch. The bugs will carry us away out here."

"OK, Mike," and they stepped inside.

"What's the occasion?" Mike said as they sat down. "I won't offer you a beer since I know you don't drink in uniform, but I do have some tea in the fridge if you are interested?"

"No that's alright; I have enough caffeine from our office coffee to keep the whole county awake tonight. Mike, this is official business and I have a few questions for you."

"Ask away, I'll answer if I can."

"First of all, did you watch the six o'clock news?"

"No, I didn't," Mike said with a quizzical look on his face. "Did I miss something?"

"An Airboat sank last night and the owner was stranded on the river." Buck watched for a reaction and saw none.

"I'd hate to be on that river at night without a boat. What happened?"

"The fellow didn't make it!" Buck exclaimed.

"Do I know him?" Mike offered with a degree of concern in his voice that wasn't in his heart. Mike's only regret was that Orin wouldn't be around to suffer the consequences of the plan he had put in motion earlier today.

"I don't know," said Buck, "that's why I am here. His name was Orin Taylor," Buck stated with his eyes burning into Mike's.

"Yeah, I know him," said Mike he's the fellow who owns the airboat *Wet Dream*. And he was at the spring the day Jimmy came up missing, right?" and Mike stared back into Buck's hard gray eyes, neither man smiling.

"That's right," answered Buck, "he's the one. Have you seen him lately?"

"Yeah, I saw him over at The Crossroads last week. Played some pool with him as a matter of fact. He was pretty good but he had to cheat to beat me." Buck's eyebrows lifted a bit at this news and Mike noticed.

"How did you know him well enough to play pool with him?"

"It was arranged by some of his buddies and from what Charlie told me, he could have been the last one to see Jimmy alive, and I thought I might just ask him myself."

"Just what did Charlie tell you?"

"Not much. Just that Orin left the Spring about dark."

"What did Orin have to say about it?"

"Nothing. He said he never saw anyone on the way home."

"You didn't see Orin last night?" Buck asked.

"I've been out of town since noon yesterday. I just got back tonight in time to meet the Banners for dinner."

"Tell me about your out of town trip Mike." And Buck reached for his notebook.

Mike said, "Buck, what's this all about? Do you think I had something to do with this Orin Taylor business?"

"As a matter of fact I do," Buck replied, "I think you suspected him of having something to do with the Thompson boy's disappearance, as I do. And you may have tried to take matters into your own hands."

Mike tried a surprised look that came off fairly good and said, "You suspected him of what?"

"I don't exactly know what, but I know he was heavily involved in Jimmy's disappearance and I think you knew as well. Now tell me about your trip," and Buck readied his notebook.

Mike outlined his trip to see Kurt, mentioning the hotel he stayed at, gave Buck the times when he checked in and when he checked out. He told him about meeting Kurt and bar hopping that night and then again for breakfast this morning at The IHOP. He said Fred at Stumpknockers could verify when he left and when he returned since it was the last place he left and the first place he went when he returned. He said he had made reservations to have dinner with the Banners two days ago. Buck asked for Kurt's number and Mike gave him a number which would relay a message to Kurt on the research ship he was staying on.

"Buck, I don't know what you're trying to prove here, and I don't know a damn thing about how this fellow Orin died or got killed or what, but I can tell you this. If he had anything to do with Jimmy's death, I'm glad he's dead, cause you weren't doing much to see him punished."

Buck's face flushed and he replied with a touch of anger in his voice, "I don't need to defend my actions to you. He was a suspect only recently and the truth would have been known if he was still alive to tell it. I can promise you that. With him dead we may never know what happened."

Mike didn't reply for a minute he just looked at Buck then finally said, "I'm sorry Buck, I had no call to say that. I guess I'm just angry you didn't tell me he was a suspect. I know you were doing the best you could to find out what really happened, and I'm sorry if this puts you at a dead end, but I'm not sorry for him if he did something to Jimmy. You said he died, but didn't say how?"

Buck told him, having an idea that he already knew, and they discussed a few details. Buck said for him to watch the ten o'clock news then excused himself, said his goodbyes and left.

Mike sat there contemplating what had just transpired. He still thought Buck was just on a fishing expedition. He was glad he had worked so hard on his alibi. He knew Kurt would do his part. He also knew that tomorrow would be the first day in the beginning of the end of this tragedy for Jim and Jenny. It would not be easy for them. But after one more phone call and one more newspaper article, the healing process could begin.

Mike could have passed his newly gained knowledge straight to Jim and Jenny but he didn't want them directly involved. Their burden in the next few days would be heavy enough without the authorities questioning them about where they got their information, and he didn't want them to have to protect him. Better that they knew as little as possible. He didn't want to chance giving the information directly to Buck, and besides he knew that the spin Robert Hastings would put on this story would be more impressive as an editorial than an after the fact news item. This was the best way and the result would be the same. He would rather Orin had lived to pay for his sins, to suffer the humiliation of public exposure. He knew that proving Orin guilty in a court of law would have been a difficult job. *Guilty of what?* Probably manslaughter at best, it certainly wasn't murder. *Obstruction of justice, leaving the scene of an accident?* Mike didn't know and didn't care. Orin was history, but Mike wanted the world to know what he had done. Mike didn't know how much effort Buck would put into proving a dead man guilty, but he thought the next article would help spur him on. Mike would make the call to Robert Hastings right after he read the paper in the morning.

Chapter Forty-three

Checking the alibi

Buck wasn't out of Mike's driveway before he was on the phone to the number Mike gave him for this fellow Kurt. He wanted to make sure he got to him before Mike did. He had to leave his cell phone number. They paged Kurt and he called back within two minutes. That was not enough time for Mike to call and brief him. Kurt backed up Mike's story 100 percent. Buck called dispatch and gave Marge the hotel information and asked her to check it out. Mike was a very good liar, but there was still that feeling in his gut and it was reinforced by the fact that Mike had been to see Charlie. He wanted that report from Gerry on the airboat. He had asked Gus to visit Orin Taylor's house and put some crime scene tape on the doors and make sure they were locked. He would get a court order for a search in the morning. He could not imagine what else he would be forced to do the following morning, until after he read the Sunday Paper. This Sunday would be like no other Sunday in his life.

Chapter Forty-four

At last!

Jim said, "I guess you know where all this is comin' from?"

"I surely do," Jenny said as she looked at him over her glasses. "I reckon I just don't know how."

"Well I don't know, but I've got an idea how, and I hope no one else does."

Jenny had been staring at the newspaper in her lap for half an hour. She had read it several times and just kept looking at it as if it were suddenly going to reveal something she had missed before. Jim had long since read it and passed it to her. He had been in deep thought since the phone call late Saturday evening. That call shook him up real bad, even worse than Jenny he thought in retrospect. Of course she had cried and he had held his tears in check while trying to force down the lump in his throat. They hadn't slept last night, just tossed and turned for several hours, finally getting out of bed and fixing a couple of strong scotch and waters.

Their anticipation of the article they knew was coming was more than they could stand even though they already knew what it would say. It's funny how the written word carries more weight, how we tend to believe it far greater than the spoken word, especially words spoken through a wire from someone you can't see on the other end. Well the words were there and they carried plenty of weight. They were afraid the words would ring true, and they were afraid they would not. The turmoil in their stomachs may eventually be replaced by a peace they hadn't known for five years, but they could not reconcile that at this time. They were up and waiting at 4:30 that morning when the crunch of tires on the gravel road and the plop in their driveway

154

announced the Sunday Paper. After having read the written words, they could only wait in anticipation of what this awful Sunday would bring. The second headline had brought a surprising twist they hadn't anticipated.

Chapter Forty-five

Double vision

Buck had his alarm set early. He knew he wouldn't have much time today. He didn't know how busy he would be. He went out and retrieved the Sunday paper knowing there would be a front page article on yesterday's accident, (if it was an accident). When he saw part of a bold headline, - **DEATH ON THE WITH** - he was not too surprised. He tucked it under his arm and carried the paper into the kitchen where his coffee was brewing. When he unfolded the paper and laid it on the table he thought for a second he was seeing double. There it was again - **DEATH ON THE WITHLACOOCHEE** - what the hell?

There were two articles, one on each side of the front page. They were two different articles by two different writers, each with the same headline. There was a good aerial shot of the confused scene around the airboat under the first one. It showed the body being transferred to the boat. It had a good bit of text and a continued on page 6A arrow. That article didn't interest him as much as the next one which was on the other half of the page. There were no photos and it had a *'To be continued Monday'* notice at the bottom. He read the article and stared at the paper in disbelief, his name at the bottom burning a hole in his brain.

What the hell was this? It couldn't be a joke. Could someone have printed it as a joke? He knew the answer was no before he had finished asking himself the question. How could this be? Orin was dead. Where was this information coming from? Was there someone else other than Orin who knew what happened? He was beginning to think he knew. He didn't know how, he just knew. "That son of a bitch!" he said out loud.

156

He picked up his phone and dialed the number of the St. Petersburg Times and asked for Robert Hastings. A cheerful voice said for him to hold while she patched him through. Ten seconds later he was talking to Robert. He asked him if this was some kind of weird joke. Asked if the editor was nuts putting two headlines like that on the front page. Robert said it was a surprise to him until it was too late. He too thought it was in poor taste but it wasn't up to him. Then Buck asked the one million dollar question, "Where is he?"

Robert gave him a precise location, "He was wrapped in plastic and buried fairly deep, under a small bush, about three or four paces east of the large cypress, the one with the eagle's nest. It was on the east side of the river just south of mile marker 17."

Buck knew this location; he had spent several hours near there just yesterday. Robert refused to name his informant, said he didn't have a name and Buck knew he couldn't force him to tell him even if he did know. Buck questioned him further to see if there was any information he didn't put in the paper and he learned exactly how Jimmy died. *Holy Shit! It was Orin,* he knew, but didn't say. Robert informed him about the call he had yet to receive with more information, and told Buck he would pass the information along as soon as he had it. Buck thanked him and hung up still partially stunned.

He snapped out of the trance and knew he had to get moving. He would deal with Mike Tracy later. He called the office and alerted Josey who had not read the paper, but had already heard about it from Bert. Bert always read the morning paper over coffee at The Front Porch. They opened at six and he made it his last stop before checking in at the office at the end of his shift. It was a little after seven now and he had Josey tell Bert to stay put, he would need him. Had she heard from Gerry Grant about the sunken airboat? Yes they had it up and floating. The only reason it sank that they could find right away was the drain plug was out. They found it loose in the bottom of the boat. There was also a loose gas line. The fuel tank was half full of gas and half full of water but the carburetor had no gasoline, just water. At first glance there was no sign of violence. Had she heard from the Hotel in Stuart? Yes, they verified Mike's check in and check out time.

"Josey, I want you to call the coroner and have him meet me at Angler's in thirty minutes. Have him call the state boys and ask for a forensic specialist to join us. Tell him we are about to dig up a body that's been buried five years. Have Bert look up a couple of shovels and be at Angler's too, then get Gerry on the radio and patch him through to me. I'll be in the car in ten minutes. If the boss calls—and he will—patch him through also."

Buck took a three minute shower, dressed in four minutes, poured himself a large coffee to go and was in his cruiser in slightly less than ten minutes. He was out of his drive when the call came through from Gerry. "What's your 20 Gerry?"

"We are about six miles upriver from Angler's with the airboat in tow."

"Good, how much sleep have you had?"

"Some," said Gerry, "What's up?"

"Have you read the paper this morning?"

"No."

"I'll fill you in when you get to Angler's. What's your ETA?"

"I'll be there in about forty minutes."

"Good, I'll be waitin' and I'll need you and your boat for a few hours. Can you line up another boat about the same time?"

"Roger that."

He had no sooner hung up when the phone rang again. "It's Sheriff Conway Buck, and he is hot." Josie replied.

"I s'pect he is. Put him through."

"Buck, just what in the hell is going on?"

"Don't get excited, Bill, I'm right on top of it."

"Hell, Buck, this is embarrassing for the department. How the hell can something like this happen? Whose giving that damn reporter all that information?"

"Bill, you're just going to have to trust me a little while longer on this one. I'm as busy as one armed paper hanger right now. I'll call you this afternoon and explain the whole thing."

"You better." Click.

Chapter Forty-six

The rest of the story

Mike was up earlier than usual for a Sunday Morning. The twin headlines had shocked him awake before he'd had his coffee. He had read both articles over breakfast, the one about Jimmy first. He had cleaned up the kitchen, poured himself the last cup of coffee and readied himself for the phone call to Robert. He made that call from the pay phone in back of Stumpys before his first run of the morning. There was usually no one around this early and this morning was no exception.

He dialed the number and the same cheerful voice that had greeted Buck earlier that morning said, "St. Petersburg Times, may I help you?"

"Robert Hastings please."

"Thank you, please hold while I transfer your call."

"Robert Hastings."

"This is your friendly informer who called yesterday. I liked your article but was surprised at the circus treatment on the front page."

"I can assure you I had nothing to do with that. I am more than a little perturbed. In fact, I may not be working here after the last article in this story appears. Using the same headline was in poor taste and I would have been happier if my article had appeared on the editorial page. But that's water over the dam and you and I have an agreement."

"You are absolutely right," Mike agreed, then began to feed Robert the last of his information. He felt Robert would do a fine job of presenting it so he kept it basically to three small but significant facts. These facts even if circumstantial would point the finger in the right direction. Robert had already explained that he could not use anyone's name and directly accuse him. But that he would implicate him as best he could.

———————

Robert started to work as soon as Mike hung up. He still didn't know his informant's name and guessed he may never know. He now knew the identity of Jimmy's assailant even if he couldn't divulge it. The shock of the coincidence was alarming. Robert Hastings thought about his informant, the cool manner he had, the seemingly private knowledge he had. He wondered how that information had been obtained and said to himself, "I may know the answer to that question." Robert's story would appear the next day in the Times.

Chapter Forty-seven

Under the eagle's nest

Buck arrived at Anglers in less than twenty minutes. Bert arrived shortly with the shovels, the coroner was right behind him. Gerry had gotten Will Langston to bring another Fish and Wildlife boat. Will was a Florida Cracker (native) he would be good help. They helped him launch the boat, had him pull it over to Anglers dock to wait. The forensic expert arrived just as they saw Gerry round the last bend upriver less than a mile away.

Buck drew the forensic expert, Elizabeth Morel and Bill Jenkins the county coroner, to one side for a private briefing. He told them the grave was five years old and got very little reaction from either one. *How could this be routine to either one of them?* He asked her to tell him what procedure they should use and she asked him a half dozen questions before she answered. She also told him to call her Liz. Her information was helpful, he didn't want to botch this up. By the time she finished Gerry arrived. Buck had noticed that Bill Jenkins had agreed with every thing she said, but had not offered one suggestion on his own. He's just a windbag, Buck thought.

Buck wanted to examine the airboat in tow but that could wait. He decided he would quiz Gerry on the way; he may have some ideas of his own.

They divided up into the two boats with Buck, Liz, and Gerry in the lead boat and both boats headed upriver on a plane. Buck briefed Gerry on the way and told him where they were going. They discussed the airboat and Gerry said the only thing that didn't add up was that the drain plug was not only out, but it was up front on the forward side of a short bulkhead. If it had just popped out it would have been behind the aft bulkhead.

"How many ways could it have gotten there?" Buck asked.

"I don't know of any unless Orin or someone else put it there," Gerry stated with a determined look on his face.

"Could it have been his spare?" Buck asked.

"I suppose, but I don't think so."

"Could it have floated over the bulkhead when the boat went nose up?"

"Buck, you know those things don't float."

"I thought maybe the rush of incoming water could have pushed it over?"

"I don't see how," Gerry said. "You need to look for yourself. I had to put it back in place to float the boat, but I'll show you where I found it," he said then continued with sheepish grin, "I guess I should have left it there but I didn't think about until I had it in place and besides I hadn't brought another one."

"It's alright Gerry. That's an honest mistake and I should have thought about it too. But you would think it would take somethin' more than a loose drain plug to sink a boat like that. It seems an awful coincidence that the gas line came off at the same time. That boat wouldn't sink with the plug out if it was on a plane. And Buck saw Gerry's face light up. "What is it Gerry?"

"That could be it Buck," Gerry said, "the plug could have been out for a long time and as long as he was moving everything was OK, but when the gas line came off and the carburetor ran out of fuel, the speed dropped and the boat sank." Gerry grinned as if he was Sherlock Holmes.

"Yeah Sherlock but that doesn't explain how the drain plug got forward."

"Yes it does," he exclaimed, "he could have pulled the plug to drain water from the bilges and just forgot about it or the gas line broke before he could put it back in."

"I'd like you to show me that trick in an airboat some-time," grinned Buck, "with that control seat way up in front of the motor."

"Well it's possible if you moved fast," Gerry said with his chin down.

Buck thought about it some while the cypress trees whizzed by. He supposed it was possible to pull the plug on an airboat and get it up on plane quickly but it sure wasn't probable, and he would have the same problem again when he stopped. Orin had been visiting his girlfriend's house on the river. If she had a lift like Orin's he could have had the plug out there and forgotten about it when he left. I'll have to check that out. He could have pulled it up on shore to take a leak somewhere on the way home and pulled the plug then.

Buck saw the big cypress with the eagle's nest way up-river, and said to Gerry, "I'll look into all that later, right now I have my hands full."

Chapter Forty-eight

Grisly job

There was a bush about four paces out from the north side of the tree, but it wasn't very small. They started digging under Liz's direction. Bill Jenkins was necessary but useless. He would second guess Liz and offer a suggestion only to be corrected with a reasonable reproach or alternative. He soon resigned himself to just watching. When the body was found, there was so little left that Buck wondered if they could determine anything about the cause of death or even get a positive identification. There were of course scraps of rotted clothing which might be identifiable and he knew they could check dental records, but to him what was left after five years in the ground offered no information. He noticed that the missing life jacket was still missing.

The digging was easy as the dirt was soft. The hardest part was separating the roots of the bush that had intertwined with the skeleton; they clipped them off where they were too tedious. They dug wide around what was left and gently lifted the remains out of the hole and into the body bag along with a good bit of dirt from directly underneath. Before they moved anything it was photographed from all angles. Liz made three or four pages of notes and a very good drawing with a few things numbered. She had sifted about three bushels of dirt through a quart size sifter and found nothing but rocks. She would have to do the same thing to the dirt in the body bag later. Bill Jenkins mostly got in the way to the point where Buck was thinking about finding him a fishing pole and sending him downriver.

It was over in about four hours and the trip back to Anglers cooled them off. They had roped off the scene with tape and left the dirt piled up. They may have more work to do here before it was over. Bill Jenkins drove off with the remains in his hearse, headed towards the county morgue. Liz had asked Bill not to do anything until she arrived later and that was alright with him. She then asked Buck to join her over a cold Coke.

Liz was an attractive woman and Buck had learned she was single. Long legged redheads had always appealed to Buck, especially if they were intelligent and Liz was certainly that. But this invitation from Liz was for an exchange of information only, for both of them. They ordered drinks and burgers and discussed the events of the day.

She hadn't found the cause of death. She would perhaps be able to determine that at a later date but it was doubtful. There seemed to be no signs of a violent death, and around water that usually meant drowning. She wouldn't be able to confirm that without lungs to check for water. The only indication of violence was that one of the left wrist bones had a crack. She had done this before and was prepared to deal with what she had found. She *was* able to control her emotions, but was still upset and Buck could sense it.

"How do you get used to somethin' like this?" Buck asked with honest concern.

"I don't Buck," she said rather flatly.

"I uh . . . I didn't mean to offend you, I just know how it affects me and I know how difficult it is to hide this. I just wondered if it ever got any easier?"

"I knew what you meant Buck. You didn't offend me," she said looking him in the eye, "and no, it doesn't get any easier—it hasn't for me anyway. Tell me about the kid."

Buck went through the details of Jimmy's disappearance told her he didn't know Jimmy but had learned a lot about him from talking to those who knew him. "He was well liked by everyone who knew him. He was good, not great in school, lost both his parents in an automobile crash on US 19 at the age of eleven or so, then lived with his grandparents on the Withla-coochee until he disappeared at the age of fourteen. His grandmother adored him and his grandfather thought he would be the next president. He was a good friend of Mike, their next door neighbor who runs the river tours—worked for him some."

"You must mean Mike Tracy?" she said with a smile on her face.

"Yes, Mike was his fishin' buddy. Do you know him?" he asked incredulously.

"We used to date a few years back when we were both living in St. Pete. I haven't seen Mike in years. I knew he had a tour business somewhere on the river but I never get down this way. Do you know Mike?"

"Yes, I know him, but not well. How well do you know him?" he said, then tried to shrink down under the table thinking he had just put his foot in his mouth. "I mean how well do you know his character?"

She laughed at Buck's awkwardness and said, "I know quite a lot about him," then forced a straight face, "Is he under suspicion? Is that why you want a character reference?"

"No, no, just the opposite. You read yesterday's paper about the body we found Saturday?" And she nodded. "That fellow we found was the guy who did this. I am convinced of that, but I can't prove it yet. Hell!" he exclaimed, "It was five years before I figured there was any foul play. Why I want an opinion of Mike Tracy is that I think he may have had somethin' to do with this fellow's death. I know he suspected this guy Orin just like I did, and I know he thought I was going too slow at figurin' all this out. I'm afraid he may have taken the law in his own hands. I have nothin' but a gut feelin' on this."

She looked hard at him, this man who was twice her age and twice her size. He had the bearing of a younger man but the strain of his job had taken its toll on his features. He looked his age but she sensed a younger man's strength in the older man's body. She thought she would have liked to have known him when he was younger. She also would not like to have him suspect her of anything. She continued, "Mike is a complicated man, Buck. He is not a violent person at heart, but yet he is capable of violence. He is not into violence for violence's sake, but I have seen him resort to violence when he thought it was needed. He does have a temper but controls it rather well. I don't know if he's vengeful. He's very protective. If someone close to him needed violence to protect them, he would be up to the job. But to take action after five years? I don't know. I'm no psychiatrist."

"Neither am I," said Buck, "I just get these gut feelin's and they are usually right."

"You think Mike may have killed this guy?"

"Naw . . . he didn't kill him. The biggest gator I've seen in a long while killed him, and done a dandy job of it too."

"Then what did Mike do, sic the gator on him?" she grinned.

"Well," Buck said, with a grin of his own, "that may not be too far from the truth."

She laughed, "I know Mike is a very commanding person at times but I had no idea he could enlist gators when he needed them." Then she added with a more serious tone, "You need to explain that one."

"He surely didn't kill him, but he may be responsible for Mr. Taylor bein' stranded on that river alone all night, and that's what got him killed."

"You sound pretty sure. Do you have any proof?"

"No, and I may never." Buck took a breath deeper than usual, as if he had more to say, paused and looked at Liz with cold gray eyes, and said, "I'd appreciate it if this conversation went no further than this table. I'd especially not want it to get back to any of our bosses."

Liz returned his solemn stare and said, "My lips are sealed."

Chapter Forty-nine

The clincher

Buck got a call early that evening from Robert Hastings, and as a result, sent Bert over to Orin Taylor's house to check out a new clue which Robert informed him of. He had suggested they look in the rafters of Orin's boat house for Jimmy's life preserver. This one would provide them with the first positive link between Orin and Jimmy, still circumstantial but a lot more conclusive. These new clues were presented to Robert by his informant whom Robert could not or would not reveal.

Bert called him on the radio later to confirm that they had found what they were looking for. He knew this would be what he needed to close this case and officially charge Orin with the crimes. Buck knew there was only one of two ways the informant could have gotten that kind of information and that was to be there first hand or force it out of Orin Taylor, and he knew the answer to that. He wasn't through with Mike yet.

Chapter Fifty

The rest of the story

DEATH ON THE WITHLACOOCHEE

Continued from Sunday

Five years ago Jimmy Thompson disappeared while fishing on the Withlacoochee River. His boat, motor and nearly all of his fishing gear were found. His body and his life jacket were never found. The reason they were never found is that someone didn't want them found. Exactly what happened on that fateful night may remain a mystery forever. There were no witnesses, no one to point an accusing finger, no one to confront this person with the enormity of his deed. There were no clues that law enforcement could sink their teeth into, at least not then.

Four weeks ago a watch was found in Blue Spring about a mile upstream from where Jimmy's boat sank while tied to a tree. This watch was Jimmy's and it provided the first truly visible indication that violence and foul play may have been involved. The watch was stopped at the time that Jimmy was due off the river. The watch had suffered a severe blow which cracked the crystal letting water in. The water in the watch was identified as river water from where the boat sank and not spring water where the watch was found. The inescapable conclusion was that someone threw it there sometime after it stopped. Someone who didn't want it found.

After the deeds were done, the person responsible for Jimmy's death buried Jimmy's dead body and hung Jimmy's life preserver in the rafters of his boat house. Whatever mystery

169

clouds this incident after the investigation runs its course will remain a mystery. The only witness is now dead. There is irony in the death of this witness in that he died on the river in a violent fashion, as did Jimmy. There is irony in his death, in that near where it occurred, was the spot where Jimmy was buried. There is also irony in his death in that there are no witnesses, and there is mystery, mystery that clouds the circumstances which led to his death. His name won't be mentioned here but some of you may put two and two together.

My article yesterday did indeed lead to the discovery of Jimmy's remains. They have been collected and positively identified. My heartfelt sympathy goes out to James and Jenny Thompson who have spent this past five years with the heartache of wondering what happened. Jimmy's death was the result of an airboat accident. His boat was swamped and he was dragged under and drowned. That in itself was a tragedy. For the person who ran him down to cover it up and hide the body was somehow a worse crime. This was all confessed to and passed on to me by an anonymous person. Circumstantial evidence has been found which supports this. Sheriff Stone said the facts presented will be verified as much as possible and the investigation closed. There remains the question of why did Jimmy die?

Jimmy died from his exposure to a situation which has been allowed to exist in spite of the common sense that screams "stop it". He died of ignorance, selfishness, and apathy. Those who operate a dangerously powerful machine in the confinement of a narrow river are either ignorant of the consequences or so selfish as to ignore the rights of others and to the danger it creates. And those who live knowingly with those consequences and either turn the other cheek or look the other way are killing the Jimmies with their apathy. The Withlacoochee River is infinitely more suited to less powerful craft in the pursuit of fishing, sightseeing, bird watching, and other passive sports. A good portion of its length is a wildlife refuge. Wildlife that is periodically bombarded with horrendous noise and strong blasts of wind from airboat traffic. The birds take flight in fear, their nesting habits relentlessly disturbed. Fishermen are annoyed to the extreme even by the more courteous drivers. The less courteous drivers have turned over canoes and frightened small children. Mix this with alcohol and you have incidents such as the one that killed Jimmy.

Jimmy was allowed to die through apathy. Yes, all those who know these things and allow them to continue are putting future Jimmies in danger. Our county and state officials could put speed limits, or a motor size limit, or even prohibit motorized craft on certain parts of the river. Ah, but it is far easier to look the other way. Those who experience the intrusion of airboats into their lives will complain to whoever will listen. But it is not enough to just complain. And it is not enough just to sympathize with those who complain.

After learning the circumstances of Jimmy's death, and realizing their own guilt of apathy, James and Jenny Thompson informed me that they are forming an organization to do just that. It will be a living memorial to Jimmy. They urge anyone who is interested in helping form this organization to call me here at the St. Petersburg Times and your name will be added to mine and other concerned citizens who would like to return the safety and serenity to the Withlacoochee River that it deserves.

Chapter Fifty-one

(Two weeks after the last article appeared)
What you don't know won't hurt you

"**I** got a feeling you're never going to tell me how involved you were with this Orin Taylor thing and I respect that. I won't ask you. If you want to tell me, I'll be glad to hear and I am sure Jenny would too. I guess you're trying to protect us as well as yourself and for that we're grateful. But we're even more grateful for the results, and even if you aren't directly responsible I know you had a great deal to do with it. Our hats are off to you. Jenny and I thank you from the bottom of our hearts. You are a true friend to us, as you were to Jimmy," and Jim Thompson stood there looking Mike in the eye.

"Jim, that's the longest speech I have ever heard you make. I only wish I had had a tape recorder for that one," Mike grinned, winked, and turned on his heel, then snapped over his shoulder, "I'm just glad Buck Stone wasn't here." He got in his pickup and roared off down the drive, grinning all the way to Stumpknockers.

Chapter Fifty-two

(Three weeks after the last article)
The funeral

The funeral was a simple one, with the immediate family there, which was Jim and Jenny Thompson. Mike was there along with a few who had known Jimmy and a few who never knew him except from the articles in the papers or their association with Mike or the Thompsons. Some were there as a statement to show support for the movement to ban the airboats as well as offer sympathy to the Thompsons. Al and Sarah Banner were there and Buck Stone came with Liz Morel. The service was short; there was no casket, just the urn with the ashes. No tears were shed. The impersonal ceremony seemed only to solidify the reality of all that had transpired in the last five years. Perhaps the most affected were the ones who had just recently become involved.

Liz in her exhumation of the grave site and subsequent examination of the remains, could not help but feel sympathy, sympathy for the Thompsons, for their loss and torment, and sympathy for Jimmy who left when his life was just beginning. Her womanhood would not allow her to look at and handle the bones of a young boy without forming an attachment. Jimmy's bones, as she held them, seemed to question her, crying out, "Why?"

Buck Stone also felt a similar attachment. His job was over now and in retrospect he felt he had let Jimmy down. He knew in his heart he had done the best he could and he felt that the Thompsons understood that, but Jimmy's image—the vision of Jimmy under the cypress tree—would be with him for a long while, perhaps the rest of his days.

The tiny church was quiet as the Reverend Mark Cramer brought the service to a close with a final prayer. Jim and Jenny filed out with Mike and waited at the door to accept condolences. Mike searched out Buck and Liz and approached Liz with a twinkle in his eye. "Long time no see," he said as he took her offered hand and kissed her on the cheek. "Hi, Buck, good to see you out of uniform again."

"Good to be out of it for a change."

"I hear you're in cahoots with these guys now," Mike said to Liz while nodding towards Buck.

"Yes, I guess I am. My career took a slight turn since we last saw each other."

"Well, I'm sure it was for the better. You're looking good these days," Mike stated with the twinkle returning to his eye.

"Thank you. You look fit and healthy, this outdoor life you're leading must agree with you." Liz smiled her eyes matching Mike's steady gaze.

Buck watched this exchange, wondering how much they were saying to each other between the words, and knowing that they must have had more than a casual relationship. But they obviously parted with respect and good feelings about each other. "You guys need to ease off a little," he half whispered, "I'm getting a little jealous. After all she is my date you know," and grinned at Mike.

"That's a fine thing, to bring a girl to a funeral on a date," Mike quipped.

"It was the only way I could get her to go out with me," Buck replied still grinning.

Liz took all this in good humor, then said to Mike, "Would you introduce me to the Thompsons?" and as an afterthought, "But don't mention that I was involved in the investigation."

"OK," he replied as he escorted Buck and Liz towards the Thompsons who were talking to Al and Sarah Banner.

Mike introduced Liz all around as a friend from several years ago when he lived in St. Petersburg, and everybody knew Buck even if they may not have recognized him out of uniform. After each of them had expressed their condolences to the Thompsons the conversation worked its way around to airboats and the river. It was refreshing for them to hear that Buck supported their efforts. They were surprised to say the least.

"I bet no one who voted for you when you were the Citrus County Sheriff knew your feelings on this matter," Mike said, smiling.

"Well, It's never been an issue," Buck stated. "People seem to take the damn things as a way of life and natural hazard in Florida same as mosquitoes and alligators."

"We hope we can change that complacent attitude," said Jenny, and several "Yeahs," were voiced.

"I can promise you that airboats on this river have seen their last days," said Mike grimly.

Buck was staring intently as if he read something ominous into Mike's words.

"Yes," Al cut in as Buck, who drew a breath as if he started to speak, hesitated, "but it won't be a swift conclusion. Laws will have to be drafted, proposed and voted on. It'll be a long drawn out process. But the opportunity is here now and we have to get started."

The conversation wound down and soon turned to fishing. Buck commented that he hadn't been fishing in years and Mike told Buck to call him sometime. Buck said, "I just might do that."

Liz and Mike exchanged phone numbers with a, "Call me sometime," each wondering if they would.

Chapter Fifty-three

(Six weeks later)
Now I know

Mike saw Buck pull into anglers in his cruiser. Buck had called him and chartered his boat for a fishing trip. He parked and got his fishing gear out of the trunk and walked towards Mike through the parking lot.

"I thought maybe you were here on business when I saw you driving that cruiser," Mike said.

"Naw," Buck offered with a big grin, "my car wouldn't start. I don't drive it enough to keep the battery up. It was just easier to take the cruiser than fool around with them blasted cables. Beside we need to be on the water at sunup don't we?"

"You got that right, let's go." Mike helped him carry his box down to the boat. "I got a live box full of wild shiners and the big bass are waking up hungry."

They cruised down river at a nice leisurely pace and stopped at the headwaters of Lake Rousseau to rig for slow trolling around the edges of the weed beds. While they were drifting to the quite purr of the trolling motor Buck remarked, "It's been a long time since I've been fishin'. I'd almost forgotten how much I enjoyed it. I guess I wouldn't be here now if I hadn't needed to talk to you in private."

Mike looked at him with a quizzical stare, and said, "I'll be damned, you are here on business."

"No, I'm here for a private conversation and it doesn't get any more private than this. I am not askin' any questions, I'm just going to say my peace."

"I've a good mind to just head back for the docks."

"Just hear me out and then head for the docks if you need to." Buck matched Mike's icy stare.

"Alright, say your peace. You paid for the time. I'll listen." Mike had that strange feeling that he was dancing to Buck's music and afraid he knew the tune. *He couldn't know anything about that night with Orin . . . He's bluffing.*

Buck's eyes left Mike and drifted down to study the deck. The carpet was starting to lift at the edge. He wondered if Mike knew? He started in a low whisper, "I knew all along you were right behind me in figuring this thing out. Hell, you had the watch figured from the minute you laid eyes on it. I was there too but just a little less eager. And I really knew when we discovered the river water inside. It was a while before you knew that. I reckon Jim told you?" and Mike nodded. "I know you talked to Charlie after I did and found out what he didn't tell anyone back then. I've seen him since then and he said he told you everything that he told me; Lord, I wish he had told me all that five years ago." Buck was still counting threads in the carpet, not looking at Mike.

Mike was watching Buck trying to see inside, see what was coming next. *How could he know? He couldn't, Kurt would never give in. He would stick to the story if they stuck bamboo splinters under his fingernails.*

"That led me to Orin and I'm sure you were right behind me, even if your methods were different and even though you didn't have all the information I did. I don't know how you got inside to Orin and I don't care. Somewhere along the way you came to the conclusion that he was the only possibility and that the probability was that there was an accident. And somehow you figured out that he was the kind of no good shit that would protect himself, no matter what, that he was indeed capable of hiding the body after he killed him by accident. I don't know how you found out all these things but I know you did." Buck shifted his gaze to Mike and realized Mike was studying him. Was that a bit of fear creeping into Mike's countenance?

He continued as he shifted his gaze to the weed bed beside the boat, "When Orin's Airboat was found on the river my guts told me he wouldn't be found alive and they were right. They also told me that you were somehow responsible. When it turned out you had been out of town since the day before I figured my guts were wrong, but they wouldn't let it go. You were good, real good but like most guys trying to outguess the law they just can't fathom the depth the law can take an investigation too, or the depth of our resources. I had one of my girls check the motel and I called your friend. He told me the same thing you did but my guts still wouldn't let it go. I have a high school friend who is a detective in Stuart and I asked him to check out your friend Kurt. Kurt is straight arrow alright, served his country when he had to and holds down an important job that is likely to make a difference someday if not now. Reed even checked a couple of the bars you said you went to and sure enough, he had been there with a guy of your description, and we even got a fix on your truck at one of them. But my guts still wouldn't let go. I asked Reed to check a little further and guess what, a routine check into Kurt's habits turned up that he didn't own a car and occasionally rented one from Budget in Stuart. They knew him pretty well. In fact the record showed he had rented one the night you were there. Now I thought why would he rent a car and then drive around with you in your truck? I asked him for a mileage check on the car. Guess again?"

Mike was silent as Buck paused and then continued, now looking straight at Mike, "It had almost the exact mileage it takes to get from here to Stuart and back or the other way around." The hair was standing on Mike's neck and the feeling he was dancing to Buck's tune was getting stronger.

Buck looked away and continued, "I took a long look at Orin's airboat, lookin' for foul play just like we did for Jimmy. I could only find one odd thing. The gas line slippin' off could happen anytime. But what were the odds of the drain plug slippin' out at the same time?" Buck didn't expect an answer and continued quickly. "That plug was out of the drain hole, and that caused the boat to sink. That wasn't unusual in itself, but it was in an odd place, couldn't have fallen there, it was dropped or thrown there and that made no sense. Orin would have had to pull it out himself unless someone was with him and that didn't make sense either. . . . It took me quite awhile to get the idea and I don't know how in the hell you pulled it off, but I know you did. There's just two things I want you to know. Just so you don't get the idea I can't, I want you to know that I can prove your involvement. I know you didn't kill Orin. The autopsy showed he died from loss of blood when the gator tore his arm off. I don't know if you knew that? He died hard." Buck looked hard at Mike and Mike thought, here it comes. And the other thing I want you to know is that I've officially closed the case and declared it an accident initiated by excessive alcohol. And by doing that I have gone against everything I have ever worked for, prayed for and lived for my whole life. In my humble opinion, if there was ever such a thing as justifiable manslaughter this is it. I found out enough about him in the six weeks he's been dead to know that no one on this earth will miss him. The earth's a better place without him. . . . One final thing, if you sneeze sideways again in my county, I'll nail you to the nearest oak tree for gator bait. Now let's catch one of them trophy bass this lake is famous for," and with that he threw the line he had baited up next to the weed bed and went silent with his back to Mike.

Mike finished baiting his hook and tossed his line in next to Buck's. He thought as he sat in silence, *I bet you would.* About that time both corks went under and both men looked at each other and laughed out loud as their poles bent and jerked, each with a heavy fish on.

The End

Withlacoochee Mysteries

By: Ron Johnson

There are three books in the **Withlacoochee Mysteries**
including the one in your hand.

Death on the Withlacoochee
Mike Tracy finds himself at odds with Sheriff Stone as he
searches the river and swamps for his friend and neighbor,
fourteen-year-old Jimmy Thompson.

Murder on the Withlacoochee
Mike discovers he is a target for a killer, and teams up with a
blind man and a gentle giant to find the man with a rifle,
before it's too late.

Withlacoochee War
The Withlacoochee River is literally ablaze as airboats burn and
tempers flair. Mike Tracy finds himself in the middle of a war and
can't figure out who's responsible for the madness.

*Each book stands alone with only the same basic characters, and
the Withlacoochee River to hold them together.*

Visit *www.riverron.com*
**Download free short stories, award winning poetry,
and excerpts from these
and future novels.**